STORIES FOR AROUND

THE CAMPFIRE

by RAY HARRIOT

**Not an official publication of the
Boy Scouts of America**

PUBLISHED BY:

**CAMPFIRE PUBLISHING COMPANY
226 EASTON SOUTH
LAUREL, MD 20724-2108**

Dedicated to all the boys who have shared fellowship at our campfires , particularly those from Boy Scout Troop 939, without whose encouragement and inspiration this book would not have become a reality.

CONTENTS

INTRODUCTION

A story told around the campfire as the coals are burning low can be the highlight of any camping trip with children. It can turn a so-so campfire into a good campfire ... or a good campfire into a great campfire. Sometimes it may be the only event remembered about the entire weekend.

I have been telling stories, primarily to Boy Scout groups, for over twenty years. On our monthly camping trips the Scouts always request a story to close their Saturday night campfire. Unfortunately, I have found very little material for campfire stories which is suitable for children of all ages. Many available stories are too long, too scary, or otherwise unsuited for telling. All this has forced me to be resourceful in meeting the desires of my Scouts. Out of necessity I have developed my story material from a variety of sources. I did considerable reading to gather subject material. I talked with many Scouts and Scouters, as well as other youth leaders. The results are a collection of stories that are specifically designed for telling around a campfire. These are stories that are simple and can be told in fifteen to twenty minutes, about the maximum attention span of the young listener. They are stories that will hold the child's interest, yet not leave him or her feeling scared.

The stories in this book can be divided into two categories. There are several stories located toward the beginning of the book that usually have sudden funny endings. They are designed to hold the child's interest until the last second. Then, by virtue of the ending, leave them laughing . . . or at least disbelieving their gullibility for believing the story to that point. These are followed by more serious stories that are within the realm of believing, yet should not leave the child feeling scared. It is probably good to mix your stories from month to month so the children will never know what kind of story to expect.

My closing note is that stories are not hard to tell. There are procedures that can be followed to make any storytelling venture a success. I have outlined these in a section called "TELLING THE STORY." I have also included some "TEASERS" to get the audience warmed up. The time spent reading these sections and then familiarizing yourself with the stories in this book will lend many enjoyable hours to your campfires for years to come.

Good storytelling!

TELLING THE STORY

The following procedures should be considered before telling a story at a campfire. Please read them thoroughly. They are your guide to years of successful campfire stories.

SELECTING THE STORY

There are many factors the storyteller must consider when choosing a story to tell to a group of children. The first factor is the age of the group. Different age groups will react differently to various types of stories. For example, children of all age groups should enjoy the humorous stories in the beginning of this book, whereas some stories toward the back may be too serious for a young group to understand. Some stories that would not scare older children may make younger children uneasy. Age also affects the attention span. Older children have a longer attention span, though not much longer, than younger children.

This leads to the next factor, which is the length of the story. Campfire stories should be kept short. A good story should last no longer than twenty minutes. This is particularly true for those stories told at a campfire culminating a long day's activities. Often the storyteller will find it necessary to condense the story to fit within these limits. Do it! It will make it easier on both you and your audience. Remember, with campfire stories shorter is usually better. All the stories in this book are easily told within these time limits.

Another factor to consider is the question, "What do you want to accomplish with the story?" Some stories are told strictly for fun while others may contain a moral or message. A campfire story is sometimes a good tool to get a point across to a young group. You'll find most of the stories in this book to be the "FUN" kind.

Finally, matching the theme or location of the story to that of the campfire will make the story more effective. A Civil War story while camping at Gettysburg would be better received than one about pirates, though the latter would be a hit at an ocean campout. Children prefer stories they can relate to their personal experiences or environment.

Keep the above in mind when choosing your story, and your storytelling will be on the trail to success.

GETTING FAMILIAR

Any storyteller must be thoroughly familiar with the story to be told. The story should be read repeatedly until all the facts are straight in your mind. Know the main characters and major events of the story, and the order in which they occur. Delete minor events if you are afraid the story cannot be told in fifteen to twenty minutes. Run over the story several times in your mind. Make sure it flows smoothly. This sounds like work, and it is, but the results are well worth it. If the storyteller appears uncertain of the facts, the audience will sense it, and the whole story will lose credibility. At all cost, avoid reading the story from the book. The children can do that themselves.

Use the Boy Scout Motto -- "BE PREPARED." Campfires are not normally impromptu events. If you know there will be a campfire, come prepared with a story. After a while your library of campfire stories will grow, and it will take less and less time to get prepared.

CHANGING THE STORY

It is the storyteller's right to change the story to suit the location or mood of a campfire to enhance the story's effect -- and I highly recommend it. My story about the Chesapeake and Ohio Canal in Maryland could just as well have been about the Erie Canal in New York. Also, changing the names and ages of the main characters in the story can have some interesting effects. If the star of the story is an eleven year old, blond boy, named Jimmy, and everyone knows there happens to be such a boy in the audience, there are all sorts of possibilities. Boys' names can be changed to girls' names for a female group. Any time the storyteller can use things to relate to the audience -- familiar names, troop numbers, places, experiences, etc. -- the chances of maintaining interest and everyone enjoying themselves is increased.

ESTABLISHING THE SETTING

Sometimes the setting of the campfire itself can greatly affect the success of a campfire story. Is the fire situated so that everyone can hear the storyteller? Children who can't hear may become disruptive. How is the fire? Generally, most stories are more appropriate at the end of a campfire when the coals are hot and glowing, giving an eerie effect. Make sure it is quiet! Do not allow the actions of some children to ruin the story for others.

Avoid distractions such as flashlights. Listeners should be instructed that no flashlight should be turned on during the story.

Finally, make sure the audience has something to focus on during the story. Often the hot coals are sufficient. Other times, I have used a flashlight with a red lens which I hold to my chin as I talk. By focusing their eyes on some object, the children tend to let their minds cast themselves into the story.

DELIVERY

Always let the audience know that you expect complete silence and attention during the story. Once this is established, a slight pause when noise is heard will normally return the calm. Don't talk in a monotone. Be involved in your story. Use hand movements, feet movements, or a quick turn of the head to add to the story. Remember, you are the artist and you are painting a picture for your audience. Provide enough description of your main characters and story location for your audience to visualize them. The need for this is lessened if you tailor the story to the area surrounding the campfire. Be careful not to be too descriptive as you only have twenty minutes. Allow the children some room to use their imagination.

Many stories are more effective if told in the first person as if you, the storyteller, were part of the story. Phrases such as "boys like you" or "with dark brown hair like Joey" will interject your audience into the story.

Be sure you cover all things that happen, to whom they happen, and where and when they happen. Lead up to the conclusion. With experience, you will be able to sense if you have the audience where you want them.

PITFALLS TO AVOID

1. Do not use stories that contain material which may be offensive to any member of your audience.

2. Try not to use characters with similar names. They will be hard for you and your audience to remember and keep straight.

3. Avoid too much coincidence. Stories that have too much coincidence lose credibility.

4. Don't lose control of the group. Disruptive behavior, such as talking or flashlights, should be dealt with immediately.

5. Telling a story at all costs. One must recognize that there are times when a campfire will not be successful regardless of how good it is or how well it is told. Examples are if the listeners are extremely cold or wet.

TEASERS

Following are several "teasers" which can be used to start a storytelling session. Most of them will elicit a moan from the audience and set the stage for things to come.

Do you want to hear the story about the dark sky?

Nah, it's over your head.

Do you want to hear a real ghost story?

Nah, you'd see right through it.

Did you hear the story about the skeleton?

There's nothing to it.

Did you hear the story about the corduroy pillow?

I don't know why not. It made head lines (headlines).

Did you hear the story about the slippery eel?

Nah, you wouldn't be able to grasp it.

Did you hear the story about the skyscraper?

It's a real tall story.

Did you hear the story about the peacock?

It's a beautiful tail (tale).

Did you ever hear the story about the church bell?

No. That's because it has never been tolled (told).

Do you want to hear a real hare (hair) raising story?

Once upon a time there was a man who raised rabbits.

JOEY'S FIRST HIKE

To me it was just a hike -- just like any of the other hikes I had taken in the past ten years as Scoutmaster of Troop 939. To Joey, however, this was something special. This was Joey's first hike as a Boy Scout. This was something he had looked forward to for months. Little did we know that by the end of the day, it would turn out to be a hike we both would remember for some time.

The Panther Patrol met at Stone Creek School at nine in the morning. There were eight of us. Besides myself, there were Sammy Stewart, the Patrol Leader, and six other boys, including Joey. The plan was to take a ten mile hike, fulfilling one of the requirements for Hiking Merit Badge. The route chosen would take us along Stone Creek to the Howard Farm, then into the hills to a place called the Witches' Playground. Once there, we would have lunch and loop back to the highway, which would return us to the school. Except for some moderately rough trails in the hills, it would be an easy hike -- good experience for a new boy, or so I told Joey.

The sky was clear and the sun was shining brightly when we set out on the trail. Sammy took the lead position and I brought up the rear. (Scoutmasters usually stay behind to take care of stragglers, or, at least, that's what we tell the boys. The real reason is as we get older, it's harder to keep up, and that's probably where we would be anyway. It's less embarrassing this way.) The rear also is where one usually finds the new boys, and this hike was no exception. In less than twenty minutes, there we were, Joey and I, at the back.

Everything was going fine. We reached the Howard Farm in slightly more than an hour. Although Joey and I were in the rear, we barely were ten minutes behind the main group. We all rested at the farm for a few minutes before continuing on the trail to the Witches' Playground. This trail led up into the hills and was a bit more rugged than the previous one. As we walked, I told the Scouts the story about how the Witches' Playground got its name.

"The Witches' Playground is a series of caves and natural rock formations located in the midst of these scenic hills. It is unlike any of the surrounding area. About 150 years ago, or so the story goes, a small group of witches lived there. They mostly kept to themselves in the hills, and the local towns-people left them alone.

It was rumored that the witches had the strangest pets. They would keep them penned up in caves in the hills, and would play games with them among the various rock forma-tions. Now and then, an animal would be seen joyfully frolicking through the woods.

As time went on, the townspeople began to fear these witches and their strange pets. They decided that for their safety the witches must be driven from the hills. Armed with rifles and torches, the townspeople attacked the witches' camp. They caught the witches by surprise. They killed them and all of their pets. The area, though, continued to be called the Witches' Playground."

About 11:30, we stopped for lunch. We were right in the middle of the Witches' Playground. The rock formations made a scenic backdrop for peanut butter and jelly sandwiches. Suddenly, our luck began to change. Sammy was the first to notice those dark clouds rapidly heading our way. The wind began to pick up. You could tell we were going to be in for one heck of a storm. We had scarcely got our gear packed and our ponchos on before it hit. It was awful dark -- thunder, lightning, the whole works. We decided to head for a cave to wait out the storm. Sammy pointed to this large one about a hundred yards away and off we ran, Joey and I bringing up the rear. It was indeed a large cave. There was plenty of room for the eight of us to stay dry until the storm blew over.

After about twenty minutes, the Scouts began to get bored. I decided that we'd do some cave exploring to pass the time. The storm wouldn't last much longer. We got our flashlights and started to go toward the back of the cave, Sammy at the front and Joey and I at the rear. The cave was very dark. Even the light from our flashlights only penetrated a few feet of the darkness.

We had been exploring about six or seven minutes when the narrow passageway opened into a large room. The air got very cool and there was a musty odor. I was about to head the Scouts back when Sammy yelled that he thought he saw something. I made my way over to where Sammy was standing, and sure enough, it did appear as if there was something in the shadows on the far side of the room against the wall. Slowly the eight of us approached it. As we neared the wall, we could make out the shape of a large animal.

"Could it be a bear?" Joey asked. If it was, it was the largest bear that I had ever seen. As we got closer we could see that it wasn't a bear. It stood about nine feet tall and was covered with hair. Its hands and feet were human-like and chained to the wall with large shackles. It didn't move. An older boy got brave and touched the beast with his hand. The body was warm. Could this be one of those pets that belonged to the witches? Perhaps it had been locked in the cave when the townspeople attacked.

Suddenly, the beast opened its eye. Yes, I said "eye," for there was only one, a large bulging eye located in the middle of its hairy face. When it saw us, a big smile came over its face, exposing big white teeth. We ran from the room in a panic, bumping into each other as we scrambled.

As we made our way back down the narrow passage-way we could hear the grunts and groans as the animal ripped its chains from the wall. When we reached the cave opening, we could hear the beast slowly making its way down the passageway. It was laughing -- laughing in a way that sent shivers up and down our spines.

Once outside the cave we dropped our flashlights and ran for the woods. We no sooner had reached the trees when we turned and saw the beast emerging from the cave. It was coming after us. After about two minutes of running down the trail, we came to a fork. I decided that it was better if we split up. Sammy took three boys and headed to the right and I took Joey and the other two boys and headed to the left.

We could hear the beast laughing as it ran through the woods. It was gaining on us. Which trail would it choose? It chose left.

Joey was having a hard time keeping up, but I stayed with him. The sweat was pouring from our bodies. Our hearts were beating fast. I didn't know how much longer we could keep this up. The beast was getting closer.

Fortunately, we came to another fork in the trail. I told the other two boys to go right and Joey and I went left. The beast couldn't follow us both. It chose left again.

Its hideous laugh was getting louder and louder as it closed in for the kill. As Joey and I ran, I wondered about the games the witches used to play with these pets. What was in store for us? Whatever it was, I didn't want to play.

I could tell from looking at Joey he couldn't last much longer. The beast was just fifty yards to our rear when we came to another fork in the trail. This was it. I sent Joey to the right and I went left. As Joey ran with whatever speed was left in his young body, I stayed back to try to distract the beast. I had to get the beast to follow me.

It didn't work. The beast looked at me with that big eye and laughed. Then it turned right and headed after Joey.

I couldn't leave Joey alone to fight the beast, so I followed as fast as I could. I knew it was just a matter of time, and not much time at that, before the beast reached Joey.

Actually, Joey was doing pretty well. It's amazing how fast your legs can move when you're scared for your life. But Joey's luck ended. As he rounded the bend, he could see that the trail was a dead end. It ran right into the side of a hill. There was nowhere to go and the beast was almost upon him.

Joey tried desperately to climb the hill, but it was too steep. The beast now was only ten yards away. There was a big smile on its hairy face and it kept laughing that hideous laugh. It could sense victory. It knew it had Joey trapped.

Slowly, it moved toward Joey, grunting and laughing all the way.

I was too far behind to do anything. The beast was only feet away from Joey.

It swung its big hairy arm. Joey ducked left. The beast swung its other arm. Joey ducked right. In doing so, Joey lost his balance and fell. It was all over. The beast reached out its arm and placed it on Joey's shoulder.

With a final smile and a triumphant laugh, the beast yelled "**TAG, YOU'RE IT**," and fell over dead. The game was done.

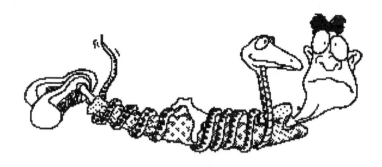

THE VIPER IS COMING

How many of you have ever repeated one of my stories after you heard it -- maybe to a friend, or to your parents? A few of you, I bet. Do you know this can be a dangerous habit? All of you are hearty, brave souls, but your friends and your parents -- now that's another story. And here it is. . . .

Billy Hodges was all excited as he ran through the door of his house, discarding his camping gear all over the living room floor. To quote Billy: "This was the funnest campout he'd attended since joining the Scouts." He didn't burn his breakfast . . . his tent didn't fall down all weekend . . . and he even managed to earn an award.

Memories of the entire campout and, in particular, the Saturday night campfire, danced in his head. He couldn't wait to tell everyone. Billy had never laughed so hard in his life as he did during the "Baby Hank" skit. He could still see Hank with that shaving cream on his face. Then there was the campfire story. The entire troop was spellbound as Mr. Arnold told of the viper and his unfortunate victims. Billy just couldn't wait to tell the world.

Billy's mother brought his anxieties to a screeching halt. "It's off to the showers for you, Billy boy!" she yelled. "How could one boy possibly get so dirty in just two days of camping?"

Sounds familiar doesn't it?

After the shower, Billy put his camping gear away and got ready for supper. He didn't mind. They were having his favorite -- pepperoni pizza. Finally, after the table was cleared and the dishes done, everyone went to the family room to hear about Billy's adventures.

Billy's dad put another log on the fire and everyone settled back, good and comfy. The entire family was there -- Billy, his mom and dad, and his sister, Dawn. Billy told it all, from the time he got to camp to the time he left. Billy always exaggerated a little, so his stories about camp were more exciting than they actually were.

After forty-five minutes of nonstop adventure, Billy exclaimed, "Want to hear our campfire story?" By this time, who could say 'no'. Billy turned out the light so the room was lit only by the faint glow of the fireplace. "Mr. Arnold always says you have to set the mood when you tell stories," Billy explained.

He proceeded to tell the story about the viper. He was part human, part snake. The viper was a true oddity. He had the physical features of a human . . . arms, legs, and all, but his skin was leathery, his eyes bulged, and his tongue was fanged like a snake. He would terrorize his victims for days before stalking them, and finally piercing their throat with his fangs. Death came quickly. The viper had this uncanny knack of choosing the right place and time for his murders. Only a few people had ever seen him and lived to tell about it. Mr. Arnold would have been proud of Billy and the way he told the story. He kept the entire family in suspense until the last second when he uttered "and no one knows who the next victim will be -- or when and where the viper will strike again." His family applauded, turned on the lights, and it was off to bed.

Billy slept good. That soft bed sure was better than the sleeping bag of the past two nights. However, Billy's dad tossed and turned all night. He kept having dreams about snakes.

"It must have been the pepperoni pizza," he said to himself.

It was the worst night's sleep he had had in a long time. "Darn Billy and that story," he murmured. He just couldn't get the snakes off his mind.

Mr. Hodges was glad to be leaving for work the next morning. Perhaps, he could get some rest -- but he almost jumped three feet high when this green garden snake crossed his path.

"Snakes, snakes, snakes!" he cried as he ran for the car.

Mr. Hodges was an advertising executive who worked on the 17th floor of an office building downtown. He couldn't wait to get to the serenity of his office so he could forget that viper and the snakes. He tried to relax in his office and look out at the beautiful downtown skyline from his window, but even that didn't work.

"The windows are dirty," he fumed. "Miss Paxton!" he yelled to his secretary, "get the superintendent to have someone come up and clean these windows."

She had never seen him this upset. Mr. Hodges was a nervous wreck when he returned home. He went to bed early, but he had another bad night. The dreams continued, only worse. This time he could see the viper -- and he was after him.

Mr. Hodges went to the office late the next morning. When he arrived, Miss Paxton handed him a note. On it was written: "THE VIPER CALLED. HE'LL BE HERE THURSDAY."

Mr. Hodges went into his office and closed the door. He knew that he was a marked man. The viper was going to get him. He tried to stay in his office as much as possible and remain calm. He was doing fine until Mr. Reynolds came in. Ed Reynolds was the newest ad writer in the firm. He wanted to show Mr. Hodges the slogan for his new ad campaign. Slowly he unfurled the poster which had written on it in large letters -- "COBRA TIRES - THEY BITE THE ROAD."

"Snakes, snakes, snakes!" Mr. Hodges screamed, "they're everywhere." He canceled the rest of his meetings and went home.

Once there, he lay down to try to get some sleep. Finally, he dozed off. The faint sound of a rattle awakened him. He listened and he heard it again: 'rattle, rattle.'

Quietly, he reached for the night table drawer where he kept a pistol. Gun in hand, he stormed from the bedroom, ready for action. Mrs. Perry, a neighbor, screamed as she saw Mr. Hodges pointing a gun at her one-year-old daughter who was sitting in the living room shaking her rattle.

He felt like an idiot. Was he going mad? He was making a complete fool of himself over this viper thing.

That night Mr. Hodges took a sleeping pill and got his first good night's sleep since Billy's story. He really looked refreshed the next morning at the breakfast table.

"I've got it," he said, "I won't go to work Thursday."

Miss Paxton already was in the office when he arrived. "You're looking much better today," she said. "Oh, and by the way, while you were gone yesterday, this man with a funny accent called. He said to tell you he'd be here today instead of tomorrow. He said you were expecting him."

Mr. Hodges had this frightened look on his face as he entered his office. It had to be the viper. He wasn't expecting anyone else. He didn't have time to think before the phone rang.

The voice on the other end said, "This is the viper. I'll be there at two o'clock."

Mr. Hodges screamed, "What do you want? Why me?" But it was too late. He'd already hung up.

Mr. Hodges reacted like a madman. He barricaded the door with furniture and told Miss Paxton he would not take any visitors or phone calls for the rest of the day.

Everything was the way he wanted it. The secretary was in the outer office and he locked and blocked his door. There was no way the viper could get in.

At ten minutes to two, Miss Paxton got a call that she was needed downstairs, and she left the office unattended.

At two o'clock sharp, the intercom buzzer sounded in Mr. Hodges' office.

"It's me, the viper. Let me in!"

"No, it can't be," cried Mr. Hodges, "if the viper can get into the front office, he can get into here." Mr. Hodges determined that he would not become the viper's next victim. He ran over to the window, dirty as it was, and jumped through.

The crowd downstairs gathered around the blood-splattered body on the sidewalk.

Meanwhile, up on the 17th floor, the intercom sounded once more.

"Hello, Mr. Hodges. Let me in. This is Mr. Valters, the viper. I come to vipe your vindows."

THE LEGEND OF CHIEF FALLING ROCKS

Many years ago, before the white man dwelt upon this nation, Indians roamed the woodlands. The Delaware tribe inhabited the area where we live. The Delaware lived in villages along the banks of the rivers of this area. They fished in the clear blue rivers. They hunted the wild game of the forest. They farmed the land. In general, they were a peaceful tribe.

In one such village lived Chief Falling Rocks and his two sons. Chief Falling Rocks was a well respected chief. Since the death of his wife, he had devoted much of his time and energy to helping his tribe. He was known for his wisdom and fairness, and his ability to get along with all men.

This was a troubled time for the Delaware. Frequently white men were moving into the area and were pushing the Indians back from their land. There were many young braves among the Delaware who wanted to fight, but Chief Falling Rocks did not believe in war. He thought that white men and red men could live together in peace. This thinking caused a big split in Chief Falling Rocks' Delaware tribe. Most of the braves and their families decided to pack up and move further west where they could resume their Indian ways without white man interference. Chief Falling Rocks and his sons chose to stay and live among the whites. They built a fine cabin and took up the white man's ways. They farmed and they hunted. There was plenty of food and game for all people to live in peace.

Everything was fine for the first couple of years, but as more whites came, many objected to having Indians living among them. One day Chief Falling Rocks left his cabin to tend to his fields, leaving his eleven- and twelve-year old sons to do their chores. Late in the afternoon, he heard noises and the sounds of gunshots coming from the direction of his cabin. As he mounted his horse he could see smoke rising from behind the trees. Quickly he rode back home, but it was too late. When he arrived, he found his cabin in ruins and on the ground were the bodies of his two sons. He didn't shed a tear. His Indian pride would not allow. But as he placed the bodies of his boys into a shallow grave near the cabin ruins, he swore to himself that he would have revenge -- the white man would pay for the death of his children.

Shortly after, strange things started happening around town. It began with the Jameson boys who had gone down to the river to fish. When they didn't return home for supper, their parents went looking for them. Down by the river they found the fishing poles and gear, but no trace of the boys.

Three days later Joey Davis disappeared while on his way home from school. All they found were his school books alongside the trail. Then there was Jesse Howard who disappeared a week later while riding his horse over to a friend's house. The horse showed up, but Jesse didn't.

Meanwhile, there were strange reports of the sighting of an Indian in war paint roaming the woods. The towns-people didn't know what to make of it. There hadn't been any warring Indians in these parts for over twenty years. Finally, when Jon Jennings, the blond-haired son of a local trader, disappeared, the people pressed for action. They organized a search party. With horses and rifles they searched the woods for the missing children or clues to their disappearance.

On the third day of the search, they came upon Chief Falling Rocks' camp, hidden in a small glen on the far side of the forest. Quietly they watched from the woods. Chief Falling Rocks was wearing war paint. Near the door of his hut was a long pole, and attached to this pole were four scalps, each decorated with a feather. Chief Falling Rocks was attaching a fifth scalp, a small bundle of blond hair, when the group attacked. In a gallop they rode down upon the small camp. Chief Falling Rocks put up a fight, but there were too many white men, and they captured him. The once quiet Indian chief was now a madman.

There wasn't going to be any trial. Chief Falling Rocks cursed and spit as they put him on his horse, hands tied behind his back and rope around his neck. With his final words he warned that the white man had not seen the last of Chief Falling Rocks and white boys would never be safe from his revenge.

"Curse you all!" he screamed.

It was over in an instant. The horse scooted out from under Chief Falling Rocks and his body hung from the tree until he was dead. The townspeople buried him on the spot and returned home.

As weeks passed, these men forgot their evil deed and the last words of the doomed Indian. Then one day, Al Walker, the twelve-year-old son of rancher Bob Walker disappeared while tending to the family's herd. There were no clues. Nothing was out of place. The only odd thing was a feather which they found near the spot where Al was last seen. Could it be?

Three months later, on the other side of the valley, Mickey Arnold, an eleven-year-old, disappeared while gathering firewood. Again, there were no clues except the finding of a feather.

One of the townspeople who had been a member of the group that caught Chief Falling Rocks remarked about how the feather looked like the ones which Chief Falling Rocks had used to decorate his scalps. Was this coincidence, or had Chief Falling Rocks returned to fulfill his curse?

Many townspeople weren't going to wait around to find out. They packed up their belongings and moved away. They moved to the north. They moved to the south. They moved to the west -- anywhere to get away from the curse of Chief Falling Rocks.

It didn't help. Bill Mueller disappeared down in Kentucky. Sam Adams disappeared two years later in Massachusetts. Phil Epstein was next in Texas. Each time, they found a feather. The legend of Chief Falling Rocks grew. As time went on, the disappearances continued, but not as often.

Over two hundred years have passed since that day when the townspeople murdered Chief Falling Rocks' sons, yet now and then, somewhere, a young boy disappears, and they find a feather.

Once in 1964 and again in 1975, young Scouts disappeared while on a camping trip -- no different from the one we're on this weekend. All they found was a feather on their sleeping bags.

No one knows who will be next. It got so that many cities and towns around the country began to erect signs to warn people -- a reminder to keep an eye on their boys.

Now I know there are many of you who don't believe a word I've said about Chief Falling Rocks and the disappearing boys. All I can say to you is this, "On your next trip by car or bus, no matter where you go in the country, keep your eyes open for the warning signs. You can't miss them. They are always placed alongside the road in easy view. The letters are big and the warning is clear: **WATCH OUT FOR FALLING ROCKS.**"

JOURNEY
INTO
THE PAST

"Why do we have to take Kevin?" Bobby complained as he got into the canoe.

"Because nobody else wanted him," answered Gary, "and, besides, Mr. Faley said so."

"It's just not fair," Bobby continued, "Kevin's such a nerd. He'll ruin the whole trip."

Gary cut Bobby short as Kevin approached the canoe. Kevin had his life jacket on wrong and the paddle he was carrying was big enough for a boy twice his size.

"Let me help you," Gary offered.

"This is going to be a long trip," Bobby muttered to himself.

Kevin was indeed a strange kid. He'd been in the troop for almost a year -- and everyone hated him. He had this unique way of getting under people's skin and irritating them to death. It probably had something to do with his home life. Kevin was an only child -- Mr. Faley used to joke that after seeing how Kevin turned out, his parents didn't want any more -- and he was spoiled rotten. His parents provided him with everything. He never had been made to do anything for himself. He had expected this to continue when he joined Boy Scouts, but that's not the way Boy Scouts operate. He began to have to do things for himself, and it was a hard adjustment. He didn't like cooking food, or cleaning up, or anything which had anything to do with 'WORK'. So it was no wonder Bobby didn't want Kevin in his canoe.

"This looks like work," remarked Kevin. "I don't think I'm going to like this. Do I have to paddle?"

"Nah," answered Gary, motioning for Kevin to sit in the middle of the canoe on the bottom.

"Two hours like that," Gary thought, "and that sucker will be begging me to paddle."

Finally everything was ready and Mr. Faley started the troop on their seventeen mile trip down the Potomac River. The clanging of paddles against the sides of the canoes echoed off the mountains as each of the eighteen canoes slipped into the water. Within fifteen minutes, the canoes were scattered all over the river.

Gary was right about Kevin. It was only an hour before he was complaining about his sore butt. Gary steered the canoe to the shore and Bobby and Kevin switched places. Bobby objected, but it did no good. Gary was giving the orders, and he wasn't going to miss an opportunity to put Kevin to work. They shoved off with Kevin in the bow, lazily dipping his paddle into the water.

"We'll never catch up now," grumbled Bobby. "The other canoes are too far ahead."

Bobby exaggerated a little bit. The other canoes were far ahead, but only a half mile or so -- and there probably were a few canoes behind them. This was typical on a river canoe trip.

Suddenly, as their canoes went around a big turn in the river, Gary had a decision to make. There was an island ahead which caused the river to fork. The main body of water went to the left, and a smaller portion to the right. Gary noticed that the canoes in front of him had taken the left.

"Here's where we make up some time," Gary shouted. "We'll take the smaller part of the river to the right. Where the river's smaller, the current is swifter, so our canoe will move faster. It's the nozzle effect." After a slight pause, Gary added, "I think."

Gary, and even Kevin, were paddling so fast they didn't notice a heavy fog was beginning to appear very quickly on the river. Bobby was the first to see it.

"Hey, look at that fog. Ain't it weird?"

It sure was. Heavy fogs are common to the Potomac River in the early morning hours, but it was now eleven o'clock. This was very strange. The closer their canoe got to the island, the worse the fog. By now they only could see a few feet in front of the canoe.

"Maybe we should go to the left like everybody else!" Gary yelled. "The larger river will give us more room to maneuver in this fog."

"Yeah," answered Bobby. Kevin didn't say a thing. He was too busy crying.

Gary tried to steer left, but it was no use. Kevin wasn't much help either. It didn't matter. Rough water caught the canoe and was pulling them along at a very fast speed. Kevin moved off his seat in the bow and joined Bobby on the floor of the canoe. Gary did his best to keep the canoe going straight -- but where was straight? He couldn't see where he was going.

When the raging water pulled the paddle from his hands, Gary also moved to the floor of the boat. Kevin and Bobby were both screaming. Gary wasn't screaming, but he sure was scared. They were completely at the mercy of the river.

It seemed like hours that their little canoe bounced around in the raging torment. Then, almost as suddenly as it had arrived, the fog lifted and the water began to calm. That was the good news. The boys stared in disbelief at what lay ahead. The river came to an end. There was no way out. The canoe drifted to the shore.

"Now what do we do?" sobbed Kevin. "I'm scared."

"Well, we can't paddle back out. There's no way against that current. I guess we'll just have to sit and wait for the troop to come looking for us."

"You forget," Bobby butted in, "we've got Kevin; they'll never come looking."

The three boys unloaded their gear and sat by the shore to wait. Surely someone would come. There were other Scouts and adults behind them. Someone else would take that turn.

After three hours, it was beginning to look doubtful. Gary realized they may have to spend the night. He ordered Kevin and Bobby to pitch the tent while he went and looked for firewood. He didn't have to go far. "Thank God, too," he thought, "I wouldn't want to go into that mess. This is the densest forest I've ever seen."

When he returned, Bobby and Kevin were putting the finishing touches on the tent. It was good to see them working together -- Bobby not complaining about Kevin -- and Kevin not complaining about anything. Maybe there's hope.

Gary was about to start the fire when he discovered that he was missing one vital ingredient -- 'matches'. "Darn, I forgot the matches. Did you bring any, Bobby?"

"No, we're in trouble."

"I've got some in my pack," exclaimed Kevin as he ran to the tent.

Bobby and Gary looked at each other in amazement. They couldn't believe it.

Kevin returned in a snap and, sure enough, he had matches. Gary lit the fire while Bobby went to his pack to get some food. It was only a bag of cookies, but those cookies tasted like steak. The boys were really hungry from their long ordeal.

As the fire roared, the boys talked of their day's adventure. They wondered what the other Scouts were doing now. Surely, they were out looking for them. Perhaps they would see the fire. If not, they'd find them in the morning. The boys talked . . . and talked. They talked about many things. They discovered that Kevin was a stamp collector and so was Bobby. Bobby couldn't believe he and Kevin had similar interests. Maybe Kevin wasn't such a nerd.

After several hours, the boys decided to go to sleep. They were beat. They entered their tent and got into their sleeping bags, but sleep didn't come. The strange noises that they heard concerned them too much. All had been camping before, and had heard 'forest sounds', but these were different. They were much louder for one thing -- and close. The next morning they saw how close.

The three boys were getting another fire started when Bobby excused himself to go to the bathroom. He hadn't been gone a minute when Gary and Kevin heard the scream. It was Bobby. They went running in his direction.

When they reached the woods they found Bobby. He was cornered by this . . . this . . . this prehistoric monster. It was much like those they had seen on television and in the movies, but Gary and Kevin didn't have time to think about it. They picked up rocks and threw them at the creature. The ploy worked. The beast turned enough for Bobby to run free. All three boys ran for the camp. Thank God the creature didn't follow.

Now what could they do? It was obvious they had to move their camp. It was too near the water, and that was a place which would be visited often by the creatures. So they did.

In the weeks to come, they would move it several times. They were getting used to it. They also were getting used to eating the wild fruits and berries which were abundant in the area, and an occasional fish they managed to catch in the river. The boys were a regular

Swiss Family Robinson -- or, at least, they were now family.

They say Scouts always will rise to meet the challenge and these boys did. In fact, Gary, Bobby and Kevin became very good friends. This may not seem like much to you and me -- but these were the first true friends Kevin had ever had. Then it happened. . . .

One day while the boys were out picking berries for their food supply, a group of small man-like creatures bearing spears and clubs surprised them. They were hairy with beards and wore clothing made from some type of animal skin. The boys tried to gesture with their hands that they meant no harm, but the creatures attacked. The boys made for the hills.

Fortunately, the boys were bigger and in much better shape than their aggressors and they were able to gain ground on them -- but they never could lose them completely. They always heard them in pursuit. Then their luck ran out. The trail ended. There was no way out. Shear walls were on three sides of them and the boys could hear the sounds of the creatures approaching from the fourth.

The boys tried to climb the walls, but they were too steep. Suddenly, Gary spotted something lying off to the side. It was a bottle, and inside the bottle there was a little man dressed in a funny outfit.

"It's a genie," Bobby cried. "Let him out!"

"This is ridiculous," thought Gary, "but so is everything else which has happened to us lately. Besides, what else can we do, with those creatures gaining on us." He opened the bottle.

There was a big cloud of smoke and a little genie which had been inside the bottle grew to a giant, twelve feet tall.

"Oh, thank you, thank you, kind sirs. I have been inside that bottle for four thousand years. To show my gratitude, I will grant each of you one wish."

"Great!" shouted Gary. "We're really in a pickle right now and could use some help. Let me see."

"Hurry up!" Bobby urged. "I can hear those creatures getting closer."

"I've got it. I want to go home."

Poof! And Gary was gone.

Without a second's hesitation Bobby said, "I want to go home, too."

Poof! And Bobby was gone.

This left Kevin who was standing there crying.

"What's the matter, son?" asked the genie.

"I want my friends. I want Gary and Bobby back."

Poof! His friends re-appeared ... and they were never heard from again.

THE BOY
WHO CRIED
WEREWOLF

Mark Kittle was bored. He had spent the entire day just loafing and reading. At least, the book was interesting -- "Tales of Horror and Suspense." Mark loved his horror stories. But, still, there was nothing to do. No excitement. 'What a lousy summer,' he thought. But what did Mark expect? Brentwood wasn't exactly New York City. It was a small town where everybody knew everybody. There was a "downtown" that was about three blocks long. It had several stores and a few alleys. The remainder of the town consisted of about a hundred single-family houses. It was your typical small rural town.

That evening Mark went over to his friend James' house to play, but the result was the same. "Boring! Boring! Boring!" Mark exclaimed. "This town is as exciting as watching paint dry."

It was on the way home from James' house that Mark got the idea. The July moon was shining full and bright in the sky. It reminded Mark about his stories -- about vampires, and werewolves, and things 'that go bump in the night.' He'd stir up this dull town. He started running toward downtown -- running and screaming.

The local residents responded to his calls and sped to his aid. "What's the matter?" they asked.

"It's after me!" Mark replied.

"What's after you?"

"I don't know. It's big and hairy -- sort of like a man -- but sort of like an animal, too. I think it's a werewolf."

The people laughed. "We don't see anything," they said.

"It's there! I tell you it's there," cried Mark. Mr. Thompson volunteered to drive Mark home. 'Boy, that's the most excitement this town's had in years,' Mark thought as he got in the car.

Two nights later Mark did it again. This time he waited on a dark street and, when he was sure nobody was watching, he took off screaming. "The werewolf," he yelled at the top of his lungs, "it's after me!" Lights went on and people came running from their houses. They found nothing -- nothing but this frightened little boy. Mark thought he should have won an Oscar for his acting. He told the people he'd been on the way home from his friend's house when this creature jumped out at him from the nearby bushes.

"It came this close," he said, moving his hands far apart. "It forced me to run for my life." He repeated his description from the previous night and added, "It's a werewolf, just look at the moon." They did . . . and it was glowing full and bright. This time they called the police.

Officer Pellucci was on the scene in two minutes. In Brentwood it was possible to be anywhere in town in two minutes. Mark repeated the story. Officer Pellucci didn't believe about the werewolf, but he was concerned there might be a stranger in town stalking children. He took Mark home and went back to search the area. Mark was really proud of his deception. Life was no longer boring.

The full moon went away and Mark's escapades ended. He'd have a full month to think of some better pranks to pull. He'd really put on a show for the town next time. He spent a week making plaster casts of two large feet with long claws. They turned out great. Mark could hardly wait for the moon to be full again.

On the first day of the next full moon, Mark grabbed a pair of his father's boots and his plaster feet, and headed for Paulson's Creek. He put on the boots and made tracks in the soft mud. He then took his plaster casts and made several impressions near the boot prints. Finally, he made sure that none of his own tracks were showing.

"There," he said proudly, "evidence that a werewolf exists. Let's see the people explain these boot prints changing into these feet."

That night Mark came screaming again. "The werewolf! It's back!" he shouted to the people. "I saw it down by Paulson's Creek. It was after me. I tell you it's a werewolf." This time they took Mark serious. They took Mark home and headed toward Paulson's Creek with flashlights and rifles.

'Darn, I'm going to miss all the fun,' Mark thought.

Sure enough, they found the tracks in the mud. "Look! The boy's right!" they shouted. "See how the man's footprints changed into the beast's."

"Wait," Officer Pellucci broke in, "that's quite a transformation. The tracks not only change from man to beast, but from left foot to right foot."

Mark had made a mistake. His game was over. The people swore they would teach him a lesson.

The next night Mark waited in the dark, waiting for the right moment to make his screaming run, when suddenly he heard a noise coming from the alley to his right. Quietly, he went to investigate. He couldn't believe his eyes. There in the light of the moon -- a full moon -- grunting and groaning, was a big hairy creature . . . a . . . . a . . . . . a werewolf!

"Oh, my gosh," he cried. "There are such things as werewolves!" In his anxiety to get away, Mark tripped and hit a trash can. The werewolf turned and ran toward him.

Mark fled. "A werewolf! A werewolf!" he yelled, but nobody came. He turned and saw that the big hairy beast was gaining on him. "Please help me!" he screamed, but the lights all stayed dark. The people had heard these screams before. Now the beast was only a few feet from Mark, grunting and groaning, and waving those big hairy arms.

Suddenly, Mark turned and ran into the street. Everyone was startled by the loud screeching of brakes and the dull thud as the speeding 1978 Chevy hit Mark. The driver never had a chance to stop in time. Mark, never had a chance, either. It all happened so fast.

A crowd gathered around the body. Officer Pellucci

slowly covered it with a blanket. Nobody thought it would end like this. It only was meant to teach Mark a lesson. Mr. Thompson took off the werewolf costume he wore. If only Mark hadn't lied . . . .

Well that's the story of the boy who cried werewolf. It's a sad story, but there's a lesson to be learned. For those who haven't guessed -- **LOOK BOTH WAYS BEFORE CROSSING THE STREET!**

A
FISH
STORY

"We'll bring back the supper," yelled David Astor as he and his two fellow Scouts, Steven Bennett and Chad Away, headed down the trail with their fishing poles in hand.

"Sure," chuckled Scoutmaster Bob Inness. He'd heard this line before. "Be careful, and be back by five o'clock," he reminded. This was the fifth day in camp and Scouts were still showing up late for supper.

Within minutes the three Scouts were standing at the edge of Lake Towanda. Slowly, they loaded their gear into the rowboat -- first the fishing poles, then the tackle box, the bait, and finally, the oars and life jackets.

"Should we put the life jackets on?" asked Steven Bennett.

"Nah," answered David; "rowboats don't tip over. Put them under the seats."

The Scouts shoved off. David Astor, the oldest and most experienced Scout, was doing the rowing. Steven Bennett sat quietly in the bow, chewing his bubble gum. Chad Away sat in the stern, his hand draped over the side, splashing in the water.

Fishing in Lake Towanda had been a favorite pastime for thousands of boys over the years. The lake was huge and contained many varieties and sizes of fish. Some boys told stories of giant fish that lived in the deepest part of the lake -- but these probably were exaggerations, just like many other stories that grow out of Scout camp.

"We're going to get a big one today," remarked Chad Away. "I just know we are. Mr. Inness will be surprised."

Forty-five minutes later, David Astor stopped the boat.

"This looks like a good spot," exclaimed Steven Bennett.

"Yeah," cried Chad Away.

The rowboat was near the middle of the lake where the water was deepest. There were no other boats around to spoil their fishing. It was a good spot, indeed.

David Astor pulled in the oars and the three boys baited their hooks and cast their lines into the water.

They were right! Within seconds the first fish bit . . . then another . . . and another. And these weren't little fish. Every one was a keeper and some were near record size.

"Wow!" yelled Steven Bennett.

"This is great!" answered Chad Away.

"Shut up and keep fishing!" prodded David Astor.

As fast as the three boys could bait their hooks and cast their lines, they caught a fish. After an hour, fish covered the bottom of the boat.

"We told Mr. Inness we'd bring back supper . . . and look! There's enough fish for a whole week."

Then they heard it!

"Let me go!"

"What'd you say?" asked David Astor.

"I didn't say anything," answered Chad Away.

"Me neither," said Steven Bennett.

"Let me go, right now!"

This time they all heard it. The sound was coming from the pile of fish in the bottom of the boat.

"If you don't let me go, there is going to be trouble."

The words came from the mouth of this big fish. The boys were astonished.

"What!" cried Chad Away.

"I said if you don't let me go, there's going to be trouble," answered the fish. "My daddy isn't going to like this. He and his friends will come to get me."

The boys laughed. A talking fish -- and one that makes threats as well. What a day this had been, a record haul and a talking fish! Mr. Inness never would believe them.

"Let's head back," suggested David Astor.

"Good idea," answered Steven Bennett.

"Okay," replied Chad Away.

"You'll be sorry!" yelled the fish.

David placed the oars in the oarlocks and began to row. Shortly after, Chad Away, from his position in the stern of the boat, noticed something strange. Activity filled the water around the boat. The boys could see bubbles and turbulence.

"Something's going on down there," Chad Away exclaimed, "and I don't like it."

"Maybe it'll stop," answered Steven Bennett.

No sooner had they uttered those words than the boat

began to rock. The boys could hear the thumping of something hitting the boat from underneath -- hitting the boat with extreme force.

"I warned you," smiled the big fish in the middle of the boat.

The thumps were getting worse, tossing the little row-boat violently in the water. David Astor started throwing the fish overboard. It was too late. With one last violent thump, the boat was tossed into the air and it capsized. The boys, with the remaining fish, gear, and life jackets were thrown into the churning water.

It was over an hour later when a passing canoe pulled David Astor from the top of the capsized rowboat. There was no sign of Steven Bennett or Chad Away. The canoe took David Astor to shore where Mr. Inness was waiting for his three overdue Scouts.

As they were waiting for the ambulance, David Astor told the story about the talking fish.

"It was awful," he said. "That talking fish was right. His father and friends did come to set him free. And those fish -- they were the biggest, meanest fish I'd ever seen. After the boat capsized, we could see them swimming around in the water. I was lucky. I was able to get on top of the rowboat and hold on. Bennett -- he almost made it. He had one hand on the boat when this giant, ugly fish with big bulging eyes grabbed him by the leg with its mouth and pulled him under."

"That was some terrible fish!" exclaimed Mr. Inness.

"Nah, that's nothing. You should've seen the one that got Away!"

TRAPPED!

The crowd had been gathered outside the old Conrad Mine for several hours. There wasn't much anyone could do but sit, wait and pray. Tommy Hampton sat on a log and cried. Two of his friends were trapped inside the mine. All he could do was wait as the rescuers raced against time to set them free -- if they were still alive.

The Conrad Mine always had been an interesting place for kids to explore. It was located about a mile outside town, off Kenner's Road. In its day, the mine was very active as miners brought the gold from down below to the surface, but the vein had gone dry over sixty years ago, and the owners abandoned it. Since then, the tunnels and caves had been an adventure for any young boy searching for his fortune in gold. Nobody ever found anything, but they had lots of fun trying. Unfortunately, the mine had fallen victim to vandals, and the authorities boarded it up three years ago.

Tommy, George and Kevin, had heard stories about the old mine from some older boys at school and thought it would be an interesting adventure to check it out. They met at Tommy's house after lunch Saturday. This was the day they would find their fortune in gold. Tommy got his dad's shovel. All the boys had brought canteens and flashlights, and Kevin, who was a Boy Scout, also brought a small survival kit. In it he had some candles, matches, rope, bandaids, candy bars, and other good stuff.

"You never know what might happen," he said. How right he was!

It took a little over an hour for the boys to reach the mine. As expected, it was boarded shut. George ran to the nearby woods and returned with a long tree branch to use as a pry. It did the trick. The boards were off in fifteen minutes. Once inside, the boys could see the signs of vandalism -- spray painted names on the walls and trash and beer cans thrown about.

They lit their flashlights and started to search for their treasure. Slowly, they edged away from the entrance as their lights explored the holes and corners of the mine. Soon, they no longer could see the light from the mine entrance at their back. Darkness surrounded them. Tommy wanted to turn back, but just then, Kevin's light spotted a small opening about five feet above their heads.

"This is it!" Kevin shouted. "I don't think anyone has explored there. It might be the gold."

This convinced the boys to stay. Tommy and George boosted Kevin up to where he could get a hold. From there he was able to maneuver to the opening. It was hardly larger than he was. Kevin crawled through on his hands and knees. His light showed that the opening led to a small chamber only big enough for one boy. Kevin yelled to Tommy to toss up the shovel.

In doing so, however, the shovel missed its mark and hit a large rock near the opening. The rock began falling -- the whole tunnel began to shake. The boys scarcely had time to run before a shower of rock and timber befell them. Kevin never made it to the opening. Falling rocks knocked George to the ground not far from where he was standing. Somehow, Tommy managed to make it back to the mine entrance. He was cut and bruised, and coughing dust -- but, except for that, he was okay. He turned to look for George and Kevin, but they were nowhere in sight. He decided to run for help.

A ranch nearby sounded the alarm and, soon, men, armed with picks and shovels, started arriving at the mine. Right off, they saw it wasn't going to be an easy task. There were rocks and timber everywhere. It was a miracle that Tommy had made it out alive. They started moving rocks and digging.

Meanwhile, inside the mine, Kevin realized that he was trapped. Although his small chamber had protected him from the falling rocks, the rocks and dirt had completely sealed off the opening. The fall had smashed his flashlight, but Kevin still had his survival kit. What good would that do? He couldn't survive for very long without air. Silently, he wondered if George and Tommy had made it out.

Actually, George lay in the dark no more than twenty feet from Kevin, but it might as well have been a mile. There was a wall of rock several feet thick between them.

A falling rock had hit George and he couldn't move his left leg. He was sure it was broken. As he lay there in the stillness, though, he could hear the dull clanging of picks and shovels. He knew the rescuers were on their way.

Kevin could hear nothing -- nothing but his breathing, which was growing heavier and heavier. He took a candy bar from his survival kit to eat. He had to think of a way to get out. He tried digging with his hands, but the rocks were too hard and the space too small to move. Besides, he had to save his energy. Work makes one breath faster -- and air was Kevin's most precious possession right now. He couldn't give up thinking. He had to find a way out. At twelve years of age, he was too young to die.

George was almost unconscious when the rescuers found him. The pain from his leg was unbearable. He was right -- it was broken. The rescuers put a splint on it and prepared him to be carried out. "Wait!" George screamed, "Kevin's up there." The rescuers turned to face a pile of rocks and timber twice the size of the ones they had just come through. It had been four hours already. How long could Kevin last?

There were cheers outside the mine when the rescuers emerged with George. Tommy was the happiest to see him. They placed him in an ambulance and took him to the hospital. The crowd sat back down to await word on Kevin.

Kevin couldn't last much longer. His breathing was getting real bad. He breathed as if each breath might be his last, and, indeed, it just might be.

"There had to be a way out," he said to himself. He could hear the faint sounds of the rescuers digging, but how much longer could he last?

Suddenly, he cried, "I've got it!"

With his last ounce of strength he reached into his survival kit and took out his matches. Quickly, he struck one . . .then another . . .and another . . . .

It was over an hour before the rescuers broke through the rocks to the tiny chamber. They were horrified at what they found -- nothing! The chamber was empty. Had George been mistaking? Was Kevin somewhere else?

The rescuers were looking elsewhere for Kevin when the tunnel began to shake again. The men grabbed what they could and ran for the mine entrance. They emerged to find the crowd gathered around a dirty little boy. It was Kevin. They couldn't believe it.

"I got out by myself," he explained. "I figured it out."

This astonished the rescuers. They never saw him. He would surely have had to pass them in the tunnel. How did he do it? How did he get out? The men pressed Kevin for an answer.

"It's very simple," he said. "I knew I had to find a way out. I couldn't last much longer. Then I remembered the matches. Quickly, I struck one . . . then another . . . and another." Kevin stopped.

"What next?" they prodded.

"That's it," he said, "everyone knows -- **three strikes and you're out!**"

51

THE MUMMY'S CURSE

New boys always are fun to have along on a campout because one never knows what to expect. Some are full of enthusiasm and some are laid back. We never know how they are going to react to the great outdoors and that first experience away from mom and dad. Troop 939 had one such boy with us on our campout to Johnson's Lake.

Greg Hall was ten years old -- or almost eleven, as he would remind us. He only had been in the troop for three weeks and never had been camping before -- not in the troop -- not in his life. He really wasn't sure that he wanted to go on this trip, but with a little coaxing we were able to convince him to try. We scheduled Greg to tent with Dennis Carlisle, a friend of his who had been a Scout for several years and was a veteran camper.

We left early Saturday morning for the two-hour drive to Johnson's Lake. The boys were their usual active selves, and Greg was no different. He fit in very well with the other boys. At camp, Dennis helped Greg set up his tent. Then it was lunch, swimming, and other activities. We had learned a long time ago the best way to keep a new boy from getting homesick was to keep him busy.

As was customary with Troop 939, Saturday night ended with a big campfire. The Scouts sang some songs, did some skits, played some games, and had a lot of fun. As the campfire burned low, the boys asked me to tell a campfire story. Actually, I would have been disappointed if they hadn't. At almost every campout for years I have told the boys a story before they went off to bed. They loved these 'spine-tingling tales of horror and suspense' -- almost as much as I liked telling them.

Tonight's story was about the "Mummy's Curse." I could tell the boys were really enjoying it. There's a certain magic about a story around the campfire. Suddenly the Scouts were no longer sitting on the sands of Johnson's Lake, but the sands of the Nile. They almost could see the mummy as it stalked its victims. They could hear the screams. After the exciting climax, the Scouts retired to their tents.

It was about midnight when a faint call from outside my tent awakened me. It was Dennis. He was concerned about Greg. Ten minutes earlier, he had jumped up in his sleeping bag and shouted, "Mummy! Mummy!" He obviously was scared. Dennis had tried to calm him down, but Greg did not respond. It was almost as if he were in a trance. Quickly, I went with Dennis to his tent, but found nothing wrong. Greg was in his sleeping bag sound asleep. I told Dennis that Greg had probably had a nightmare, and for him to go back to sleep.

"Going to have to take it easy on those campfire stories," I said to myself as I walked back to my tent. I knew that it was a nightmare, but did Greg have it, or did Dennis dream that Greg had it?

The scream an hour later told me it was Greg. Again, unmistakably in Greg's voice, came two loud yells -- "Mummy! Mummy!" This time when I got to Greg's tent there was a crowd waiting. The screams had awaken the entire troop. On checking the tent, I again found Greg sound asleep. 'Another nightmare,' I thought, but there was no convincing the other boys. They swore that the mummy was out there -- somewhere -- waiting. I saw there was no way I was getting this crew back to sleep, so I built a little fire. There we sat, nobody saying a word.

Have you ever sat quietly in the dark? You hear many eerie sounds. Sounds that probably always were there, but your senses never responded to them. Sometimes, you even think you see things moving in the shadows. So it was this night.

Suddenly, there was a sharp movement in the woods to our right.

"The mummy! The mummy!" yelled the boys.

"No!" I said, "probably just some animal." 'It had to be,' I said to myself. Even I wasn't sure anymore.

I couldn't believe it. Here I was sitting around the fire with all my experienced Scouts looking for mummies while my newest Scout, Greg, was sound asleep. Needless to say it was a long night, but we all managed to survive. There only were three more mummy attacks, all of which proved to be false alarms.

When Greg awoke, he was really surprised to find us all sitting around the fire. He remembered nothing of his screams. He mentioned that he did feel a little homesick when he returned to his tent after the campfire, but remembered nothing after that.

The Scouts wasted no time in breaking camp -- they didn't buy this nightmare stuff! The mummy was after them -- and that was that.

You almost could sense relief in the cars as we headed home. It was a quiet ride as the Scouts caught up on their lost night's sleep. Thank God, Greg was awake to talk to me or I might have joined them. Greg said that other than being a little homesick, he really had enjoyed his first campout. He was sorry if he had caused all that commotion last night, but he really couldn't remember.

The parents all were waiting when we pulled into the church parking lot, and Greg was the first to leave the cars.

"Mummy! Mummy! Mummy!" he yelled as he ran open-armed toward his mom and dad. "I missed you so much."

The other boys and I looked at each other.

SEARCH FOR THE BLACK CASTLE

Pierre Du Bois had got his wealth by devious means, among which were murder and theft. He was an evil man. His fortune included paintings by the world's most famous artists, jewels and precious metals -- gold and silver. But, for all his riches, Pierre Du Bois was not a happy man. He feared for his life. Many people were after him for revenge of his evil deeds, and many more wanted his treasure for themselves.

Because of this, Pierre Du Bois decided to take all his wealth and build himself a castle somewhere where nobody could find it. There he could be safe and could enjoy his treasures in privacy. So it was that Pierre built a castle, somewhere in the deepest, remotest part of Alaska. It was a magnificent structure. Pierre Du Bois had it done entirely in black stone -- a fitting color for this evil man.

When Pierre Du Bois completed the castle, he moved all his treasures into it and nobody ever heard from him again. Thus began the legend of the Black Castle and its treasures.

Over the years many people have searched for the Black Castle -- several have never returned. Supposedly, only one person, a young Indian boy, ever had seen the Black Castle itself, and he went instantly blind.

Karl Johnson was a devious man himself. Driven by greed, he was determined that he was going to find the Black Castle and claim Pierre's treasure as his. He arrived in Anchorage one Tuesday evening and began frequenting the local drinking establishments to gather information about the Black Castle. Nobody seemed to know anything, or, if they did know, they weren't telling. In fact, whenever Karl would bring up the subject of the Black Castle, people would get quiet and move away from him. Some said the Black Castle was evil and would not talk about it. This made Karl more determined than ever. He decided to try money.

"One thousand dollars to anyone who will take me to the Black Castle," Karl boasted, but he had no takers. Obviously, people valued their lives more than his money.

Karl was almost ready to give up his search when late one Friday evening in a run-down tavern on the far side of town the bartender directed him to an Indian sitting in the dim light in the corner of the bar. The Indian was very old and, from the dark glasses that he wore, was apparently blind. He wore a gold medallion with a red inlaid stone around his neck. The bartender said that his name was Agami. Karl walked over.

"I understand that you are looking for the Black Castle?" Agami asked.

"Yes."

"Well, stop this nonsense and go away!" Agami admonished in harsh tones.

"The castle is evil. It's cursed! Trust me. I have seen it. It is the last thing I have ever seen."

"Then you must tell me where it is."

"No!"

"I will give five thousand dollars to you to tell me. I beg of you, tell me!"

The Indian sat quietly for what seemed like hours, but, in reality only was minutes. Then he turned and spoke.

"I do not want your money. If you want to go, I will take you there. But I warn you, you may never return."

"But how can you take me there? You're blind."

"Yes, I'm blind, but I will never forget that place. See this medallion that I wear around my neck. It will guide me there. It, too, is evil, and longs to return to the place from where I took it in my youth."

"Great! Let's go!"

Early the next morning Karl met Agami in front of the tavern. He had a dog sled and a fresh team of huskies. They loaded the sled with supplies -- shovels, an axe, sleeping gear and enough food for a week. Agami cleared a seat on the sled and pointed to the north.

"Mush!" Karl shouted. With a crack of the whip they were off.

For four long days they headed north through dense woods and high mountains. Often Karl thought they were lost, but Agami would hold that gold medallion with the red stone in his hand, and quietly mumble, as if he were talking to it. Then he would raise his hand and point, and the dogs would run off again.

For two more days they journeyed deeper into the wilderness. Karl was beginning to get impatient, and, besides, supplies were getting low.

"How much longer?" Karl yelled at Agami.

Agami smiled and replied, "Not long," all the time cradling the medallion in his hands.

"What's with that medallion anyway?" snapped Karl. "Why do you always talk to it?"

"This," answered Agami, raising the medallion from his neck, "is the key to the treasure. It once belonged to Pierre Du Bois and, like him, it is evil. It is a truth stone. Ask it a question and it will always tell you the truth, but the answer will not always be as simple as it seems. This evil stone should be returned to the Black Castle."

The next day Karl again lost his patience and demanded, "How far is it?"

Agami grasped the medallion and pointed to a hill less than a quarter of a mile ahead.

"Less than a mile in that direction."

Quietly, Karl withdrew a pistol from his pack and walked toward Agami.

"I don't need you anymore," he said as he squeezed the trigger twice. Agami slumped to the ground.

Karl moved forward and started to remove the medallion from around Agami's neck. In one final gasp, Agami moaned, "Beware! It is evil!" Then he died. Karl placed the medallion around his neck and proceeded on foot toward the hill. When he reached the crest, he slowly peeked over the top. There it was, the Black Castle, in all its evil splendor. The stories were true!

A loud rumbling sound interrupted his exuberance. The earth began to tremble. He turned in time to see the ground open beneath his sled. In an instant, the earth swallowed the sled, the huskies, and Agami. Then, as suddenly as it had opened, the ground closed and the rumbling ceased.

Karl was alone, but what did he care. He had found the Black Castle and now the treasures would be his. He made his way to the castle. It was made entirely of black stone. The only entrances were two wooden doors located next to each other in the front of the castle. Next to the doors was a sign that read: "OPEN THE WRONG DOOR AND YOU WILL PERISH."

'What shall I do?' Karl thought. Then he remembered the medallion -- the truth stone. He grasped the medallion from around his neck and asked, "How do I enter the castle?"

A voice responded, "Choose the right door and you shall live, otherwise you shall die."

"I already know that," Karl fumed. Then he remembered Agami had told him that the stone's answers were not always what they seemed. He pondered the stone's words in his head.

"Of course!" he exclaimed, "I've got it. Choose the right door. Don't choose the left door."

Opening the door on the right-hand side, Karl entered the castle. It was dark and musty on the inside. Karl took a flashlight from his pocket. There were lots of cobwebs, and dust covered everything. He could see that the place was very large with many chambers, but there was no sign of the treasure. Not wanting to risk any more traps like the doors, Karl grasped the medallion and asked, "How can I find the treasure?"

The voice answered, "To reach the treasure you must go step by step."

Another stupid answer.

"Wait -- step by step -- that must mean stairs."

Karl moved the beam of his flashlight around the room, and, sure enough, in the corner there were some stone steps leading upward. Quickly, he made his way to the corner and proceeded slowly up the stairs.

At the top of the stairs Karl entered a large hall. It was very long, but at the end Karl could make out a bright light -- a bright yellow light -- twinkling in the distance.

'This is it. The treasure room,' Karl thought as he raced down the hallway. The light was so bright it had to be the twinkling of gold and jewels. He turned off his flashlight and headed for the glow.

Karl was only a few feet away from the room at the end of the hall when he realized the light wasn't from jewels and gold, but from six large candles. He stopped in his tracks, for there, on a table in the midst of the candles, was a coffin -- a black coffin.

Before he could think, a large gust of cold air hit his face. It stirred the dust and made it hard to breath. He took to a fit of coughing to clear his lungs. It was then that he noticed the coffin beginning to rise from the table. It was floating in midair -- and coming directly toward him. He turned and ran.

HACK, COUGH.

Karl could hardly breath from all the dust when he reached the end of the hall where the stairs had been -- yes, I said had been -- for now they were gone. The hall was a dead end -- no pun intended -- and the coffin kept getting closer and closer.

HACK, COUGH.

Karl was in a panic. His heart was pounding a mile a minute and his body was in a cold sweat. He slithered low against the ground in the corner. He had to do something fast. The coffin was only feet away.

HACK, COUGH.

Then Karl remembered the medallion. Quickly, he took it in his grasp and, coughing on the dust, yelled, "How can I stop this coffin?"

The voice answered, "Take a Luden's wild cherry cough drop!"

Nobody heard from Karl ever again.

REVENGE
OF THE
BUNYIPS

Some troops have their snipe hunts where they send the Scouts into the woods with their sacks for hours on end, trying to catch those elusive little creatures. Our troop is a little different, we have bunyips.

I don't remember exactly how bunyip hunts got started, but I believe it goes back to the early 1970's. Two of our Scouts, Brian and Kevin, who were brothers, returned from Australia. They made up this story about a creature which was small, but ferocious. It had long claws, sharp teeth protruding from the sides of its mouth, and gave out a hideous cry when it chased its prey -- humans. It also had only one eye, located in the middle of its head. The eye was large in proportion to the rest of its features and it had a red glow when viewed in the dark. The Scouts explained that most people had never seen a bunyip because they were nocturnal, coming out only at night. Also, flashlights terrified them. If a bunyip saw one, it was liable to attack, so it was best that Scouts leave them at camp.

Typically, the boys would announce on a campout that they were going to have a bunyip hunt. They'd explain to the new boys what a bunyip was, and give everyone a burlap sack. The new boys always were thrilled. They'd be famous. They'd be the first people ever to bring a bunyip back alive.

Of course, a few of the older boys always would go to the hunting area ten minutes early to act as bunyips. They'd wear dark clothes, so as not to be seen, and carry flashlights with red cellophane taped to the lenses. This provided a red glow to look like a bunyip's eye when turned on. When the "hunters" approached, the boys would turn on their "eyes" and make weird noises. The Scouts would spend hours in the woods hooting and hollering, and burning off energy. It was a lot of fun.

Each time there was a bunyip hunt, there usually were only two or three boys who were not "in" on the activities. The Scouts always exaggerated so much that I doubt even these boys believed the story when the hunt started. But what boy ever turned down the opportunity to run around in the dark screaming his fool head off?

These bunyip hunts took place a couple of times a year for several years. The boys really looked forward to them. It got so that several older boys would plan the event several weeks in advance. They started to get creative. There would be flying bunyips which would come jumping down from a tree. In reality, they were no more than a flashlight with red cellophane attached to a guide wire. On every bunyip hunt the older boys tried to outdo themselves with their ingenuity and creativeness. This was all right until that campout at Sherando Lake!

It was June and we had several new Scouts camping with us for the first time -- the ideal time for a bunyip hunt, the older boys thought. They spent Saturday afternoon in the woods making preparations. They picked out their hiding places and set out trip wires tied to tin cans full of rocks to make noises. They even set up a couple of "flying bunyips." They were ready. This would be the best bunyip hunt ever.

Shortly after dark, they rounded up the Scouts and told them there was going to be a bunyip hunt. The older boys instructed the Scouts to leave their flashlights on the table, and to get a sack from the pile nearby. Ronnie would lead them to the hunt area. They did as instructed.

The other adults and I sat around the campsite and talked. We could hear the yelling and screaming coming from the woods. Little did we know that the older boys had planned another prank for tonight's hunt.

The boys had been gone about thirty minutes when Billy came running out of the woods screaming.

"Mr. Samson! Mr. Samson! Eric's hurt. The bunyips got him!"

Several other boys soon followed. They were carrying Eric. They brought him down and laid him on the picnic table so I could check him. He was moaning in pain. I could see by the light of the lantern that something had ripped his shirt to shreds. I also could see some of the funniest-looking blood I'd ever seen. I was furious. Eric was joking.

Enough was enough. I scolded Eric on the spot. "Injuries are a serious business," I beckoned. "It's no joking matter. I'm very disappointed in you, Eric." I sent an adult to the woods to bring back the other boys. The game was over.

It was twenty minutes before the rest of the boys began drifting back from the woods. Some younger ones were really scared. "How's Eric?" they asked.

"Oh, he's okay," I replied.

Eddie, a new boy, obviously was shaken by the ordeal. He was almost crying.

"Are you sure he's okay, Mr. Samson? He looked pretty bad up there on the hill."

"He's fine, Eddie. He was just fooling. The whole hunt was fake. There are no such things as bunyips."

"But I saw them! They were all over the place up there. I saw their red eyes!"

"They were only make-believe, Eddie. Believe me."

"You're just saying that so I won't be scared, aren't you?" Eddie countered.

I could see there was no convincing Eddie. I was furious at the older boys. I called a leaders' meeting. The boys sat there knowing what was coming. They'd been around me long enough to know when something upset me. I gave them the whole speech -- about fun is fun, but when the aim of the game is to scare boys out of their wits, it is no longer funny. They should have known better than to pull a prank like the one they did tonight. They should have, at least, checked with me first. I would have ended it before it started. I think they got the message. They were really sorry.

I was still mad when I went to sleep that night. I hoped the older boys had learned their lesson. If there's one thing I can't stand to see, it's the older boys picking on the younger ones. With all this going on inside my head, I had a hard time getting to sleep.

I was awakened in the middle of the night by a strange feeling -- that feeling that Scoutmasters intuitively have when something's not right. I listened. I thought I heard some strange noises coming from the other side of the campsite. Quietly, I slipped on my pants and sneakers, took my flashlight, and went outside. Without turning the flashlight on, I looked around. Everything appeared normal. Then I saw it -- or them. Toward the far side of camp, near the woods, I saw faint red lights close to the ground.

"Darn those kids," I thought, "hadn't they learned their lesson?" My adrenaline was flowing. I was determined to catch the culprits. This was no longer funny. "They'll do KP for a year when I catch them!"

I slowly moved across the campsite, being careful not to make a sound. I could hear movement in the grass and trees nearby. I noticed a faint red glow from near Jesse's tent. It was coming my way. I ducked and waited behind a big oak tree.

'Two can play this game. He'll jump out of his pants when I surprise him,' I thought.

I could hear him getting close. I turned on my flashlight and jumped out, yelling "Gotcha!"

I expected to see one of my boys, but what I saw were two of the ugliest looking creatures I had ever seen in my life. Their huge white teeth gleamed in the light of my flashlight, and their one big red eye was staring right at me. "My gosh! They're real! Bunyips are real!" I screamed. There was nothing to do but turn and run. The two creatures were in fast pursuit. I made for the woods. Now there were at least five glowing red lights coming after me. I ran and I ran, but I could tell the little creatures were gaining on me. They moved fast through the woods. They didn't have to duck tree limbs and jump rocks like I did. Within five minutes, the woods was crawling with them. They were on the ground . . . in the trees . . . everywhere. I continued running.

Once I thought they had me for good. I tripped over a big rock and lost my sneaker. I didn't have time to put it back on. I just left it, and kept running.

They were all around me. They could have torn me to shreds at any time, but, instead, they chose to pester me -- like little gnats flying around your face on a summer picnic. I constantly had to dodge creatures, which were coming at me from every direction.

Finally, I couldn't run any longer. I stopped in this big clearing. There were bunyips everywhere and they were moving in for the kill. I knew I was a goner. They were coming closer and closer.

Suddenly, a large bunyip appeared in the middle of the clearing, nearby. He raised his big hand and the others stopped. Obviously, he was a leader of some sort.

"Show this man respect!" he bellowed.

"Oh, no. Bunyips can talk." I couldn't believe it.

"If not for him, you wouldn't exist. Young boys would not prey upon you. You would not enjoy the fun of their hunts. Let him go, I say."

The bunyips voiced a few dissenting growls, but, slowly, backed off. Another signal from their leader and they turned and scampered back into the woods. I collapsed from exhaustion.

I awoke the next morning in a cold sweat in my tent. The whole thing must have been a dream.

"Darn those Scouts and their bunyips!"

I could hear the sounds of the boys, already up, getting breakfast ready.

'I'll give them a hand when I get dressed. Now, where'd I put that other sneaker?'

THE GHOST OF JIM BRANNIGAN

Jim Brannigan was a mountain of a man -- a true outdoorsman. He lived with his wife and twin sons, Rod and Sean, in a cabin by Silbey Creek. The cabin was nothing fancy, but it was his, built with his own two hands. Jim made his living as a trapper. He set and baited his traps, skinned the animals, prepared the hides, and sold them to local dealers. He also hunted game for his family to eat and had a small garden for raising vegetables.

Rod and Sean were Jim's pride and joy. They often accompanied him as he set his traps or went hunting. Jim and the boys spent many hours together fishing in the creek. He was a good husband, a good father, and a good friend to all who knew him.

One day while Jim was checking his traps, he noticed dark clouds rapidly moving his way. The winds were picking up and he could sense thunder and lightning in the distance. He knew it was just a matter of time before it reached him, so he began to look for shelter. About a hundred yards away, he found a small spot beneath some overhanging rocks which would keep him dry. He reached it just in time. The sky opened up and the rains came down. The storm only lasted two hours, but what a storm. Jim had never seen it rain so hard and so fast in such a short time.

As he returned to his cabin, Jim had this strange feeling that something was wrong. The closer he got to his cabin, the stronger the feeling. Suddenly, Jim heard a loud noise. It was the sound of rushing water and crashing trees. The quiet waters of Silbey Creek had turned into a raging torment. The storm had caused a flash flood -- one of the most feared of natural disasters.

Quickly, Jim struggled to his cabin. It was in shambles, destroyed by the onrushing waters. He could find no trace of his family. He only could hope they had time to make it to high ground before the flood. He searched the area, but found nothing. For two days he searched, as the flood waters subsided.

It was on the afternoon of the second day he found Sean, about a quarter of a mile from the site of the cabin. His twisted body was among the debris washed up on the shore. A day later he found the bodies of his wife and other son. The raging waters had claimed them too. Jim buried his family in a small plot near a cluster of trees to the rear of the cabin ruins.

His neighbors tried to console Jim, but it was no use. Jim became very quiet and withdrawn. He could not adapt to being alone. He had lost the most precious things in life to him, and he could not go on without them.

On September 20th, the twins eleventh birthday, Jim gathered some wildflowers and placed them on the graves. He turned once to curse the creek, put a pistol to his head, and pulled the trigger. The neighbors who found the body buried him next to his wife and sons.

Over the years, the cabin rotted and the area became overgrown with weeds and vegetation. Then one day in 1973, a group of Boy Scouts on a hike stopped for lunch alongside the creek. Two Scouts, taking advantage of the free time to explore, came across the ruins of the old cabin. Although some boys had hiked this trail several times before, they never had noticed that the ruins were there. Whoever had made this cabin had done a good job. Most of the wood was rotten beyond use, but the foundation was still in good shape.

On the way back to town the boys tried to convince their Scoutmaster it would be a good project for the Scouts to rebuild the cabin. It would be ideal for weekend camping trips. The Scoutmaster decided the plan had some merit, and began to check out the necessary details.

A trip to city hall revealed that the local bank owned the land. The bank was more than willing to let the Scouts proceed with their project. They drew up a lease for $1.00 per year, and even agreed to donate some building materials. Things were beginning to look up. Many other local merchants donated supplies, and, before they knew it, the project was underway.

The Scouts spent every free hour at the creek rebuilding that cabin. Everything was fine for about two weeks, then strange things began to happen. Work the Scouts had completed the night before, would be undone by morning. Supplies would be broken or missing. At first, everyone thought it was the work of vandals -- non-Scouts from town. This only succeeded in getting the Scouts to work harder on the project. However, as the project progressed, the occurrences became stranger and stranger. Tools which were put down for a second disappeared, and there were no other workers in sight. Work became undone right in front of their eyes. It was almost as if someone -- or something -- did not want this cabin to be rebuilt.

These strange occurrences led the Scoutmaster to go to town to do a little research on the cabin. It was on this trip he learned of the story of Jim Brannigan and his family at the local archives. "Had the ghost of Jim Brannigan caused these occurrences?" he asked himself. "No. There are no such things as ghosts."

On his next trip to the cabin, he decided to see if the troop could locate the graves and check out the story. Sure enough, behind the cabin, near a cluster of trees, the boys found several mounds of dirt with rocks neatly arranged. Of course, the area was now completely overgrown with weeds and run down.

A few of the Scouts took it upon themselves to clear out the weeds and straighten up the area. The boys even made a little grave marker with the words *Brannigan Family* on it. The Scouts put the marker in the middle of the tiny graveyard and placed wildflowers on the graves.

The next day, a funny thing happened. When the Scouts arrived to begin their day's work, they found all the tools that had disappeared neatly stacked on the front porch. Some of the boys swore that even more work had been done on the cabin since they had left the day before.

From this point on, the troop made real progress on the cabin. It was almost as if the Scouts were receiving help from an unseen friend.

"Maybe there are such things as ghosts?" the Scoutmaster now wondered.

Finally, the troop completed the cabin. All the boys knew that they couldn't have done it without the help of Jim Brannigan -- or, at least, his ghost. By now, even the Scoutmaster was a believer!

The first campout at the cabin yielded a real surprise. When the Scouts arrived, they found a large pile of firewood next to the fireplace. It appeared as if Jim had adopted the boys in place of the family he had lost. Since then, the stories about Jim became part of the troop. There were many cold mornings when the troop awoke to a warm fire that had mysteriously built itself. Others when the leaders found a hot pot of coffee on the stove. Then there was the time a boy got lost, but "Jim" showed him the way back to the cabin. For three years, Jim was a real friend to the troop.

Then it happened. The Scouts were at the cabin for a weekend of camping. Everyone was sleeping inside due to the rain. There were sleeping bags everywhere. It started with banging and clanging. The loud noises startled the boys. Then pots and pans came flying across the room, followed closely by other objects. It was as if someone -- unseen -- was throwing them. This scared the Scouts. Obviously Jim Brannigan was mad. But why? For some reason, he was taking out a vengeance on the boys. For safety's sake, the Scoutmaster made the boys leave the cabin. They put on their ponchos, took whatever gear they could carry, and headed out into the rain. The leaders urged the boys to move as fast as possible. Objects continued to fly at them, even as they headed up the trail. None of the objects hit the boys, but they came close enough to show Jim meant business.

What had brought this sudden change in Jim?

What had the Scouts done?

The Scouts no sooner had made it to the top of the hill when they heard the roar. Silbey Creek had again swollen its banks and was storming down the valley. They could hear the crashing of the trees and the gushing of the waters. There was a loud crash as this wall of water and debris smashed into their cabin, barely a quarter of a mile below them. The Scouts returned to their homes that night knowing that, if it had not been for Jim, the flash flood would have killed everyone.

Everyone decided it was not a good idea to rebuild the cabin again. It wasn't safe in that location. This was a hard decision because the boys would miss Jim. His ghost had been a real friend these past few years. It just wouldn't be the same, camping without him.

On the next campout, the troop arrived Friday evening ... set up camp ... and went to bed. In the morning when they awoke, a large pile of firewood next to this small fire surprised them, and on the fire was a pot of coffee. Jim was back.

And they were glad to have him!

THE UNKNOWN SOLDIER

Jerry Martin had been looking forward to this campout for a long time -- a weekend of camping at Gettysburg National Historic Park in Pennsylvania. Jerry had been a Civil War enthusiast for as long as he could remember. His room was decorated with Civil War memorabilia: Confederate flags, pictures, bullets, even an old cannonball. After all, his ancestry included many who had fought in that great war, on both sides. And now, at the age of fourteen, he would be camping in the very spot where the hills once were alive with the sounds of battle. He would be hiking the same trails traveled by the Blue and the Gray. This was a dream come true for Jerry.

Why, then, was he having second thoughts? Why did he have this fear -- this feeling of impending doom?

I first noticed the change in Jerry in my truck on the way to Gettysburg. He never was this quiet. Jerry always was in the middle of things, fooling around with the other Scouts in the truck. But not this time. Jerry just sat there. Even when we set up camp at Gettysburg, he was not himself. Finally, I pulled him aside to see if anything was wrong. I was not prepared for what he had to say.

"I'm scared, Mr. Nelson," he said. "For the past week I've had this terrible feeling, and every night it gets worse and worse."

Jerry had this scared look and was sweating as he talked.

"I've been having dreams about the war ... the fighting ... the killing. It all seemed so real, as if I were there. This may sound funny, but I didn't want to come on this campout. Something's going to happen, I know it. My mom says it's all nerves -- because I was excited about the campout -- but I'm not sure. My dad wanted me to come. He knows how much I've studied the Civil War -- our family heritage and all that. He thought it would be a good experience for me. So did I until last week, but now this place scares me. It can't be nerves. I've been to other battlefields before -- Manassas . . . Antietam -- and I've never felt like this. Mr. Nelson, something's going to happen!"

I tried to calm Jerry down the best I could. He needed some reassurance that everything was okay. I decided to keep a close watch on Jerry until we went to bed.

At around two o'clock in the morning I was awakened by a scream. It was Jerry. I ran quickly to his tent.

"What is it, Jerry," I asked, "another nightmare?"

"Yes," he said, "but more life-like than before."

He remembered seeing himself wearing a uniform of Confederate gray. Then came the noise -- cannonballs exploding, gunshots, the clanging of metal. When he looked down, blood covered his gray uniform. The next thing he knew, he woke up screaming. I talked to Jerry for awhile, again trying to calm his fears. I kidded him about his Civil War hobby and how he had become too involved with it.

"Why couldn't you collect coins or stamps?" I asked.

I stayed with him until he fell asleep.

Jerry was doing much better at breakfast, but he still was scared about going on the trail. He was sure something would happen. I told him to forget such nonsense and promised that I would stay with him all day. Jerry really perked up when we toured the museum in the Visitor's Center. He marveled at all the Civil War relics and wished they were in his collection. Once outside, however, he began to feel uneasy again. He didn't say anything, but I could tell he was scared. He stayed by my side, away from the other boys. While most of the Scouts were looking at the monuments and statues, Jerry scanned the landscape and old houses.

"Mr. Nelson, I feel like I've been here before."

I let the comment pass.

Soon we approached Cemetery Ridge, scene of some of the fiercest fighting of the battle. This was the site of the famed Pickett's Charge where the Confederate Army made a valiant effort to break through the Union line. Jerry stopped and grabbed his ears.

"The noise! The noise!"

"What noise?"

He looked at me in a puzzled way and said nothing. I could sense that something was going on inside his head. He took his hands away from his ears, and we moved on.

Suddenly, a few minutes after we reached the ridge, Jerry grabbed his side and fell to the ground in obvious pain.

"What's the matter, Jerry? What's the matter?" I asked in a panic.

"I'm bleeding! I'm bleeding!"

Slowly, I moved his hands away and checked his side. There was no blood. Jerry had that strange look in his eyes again. Enough was enough. I turned the group over to one of my assistants, and took Jerry back to camp. He felt better now.

The rest of the group arrived around supper time. Shortly, after we had eaten, Jerry started to complain about his stomach again. He did look very pale. I felt his head. He was running a fever. I instructed him to lie down in his tent.

"No!" he shouted.

"No tents! I'll die in a tent!"

He was almost hysterical.

"Okay," I said, and fixed him a spot to sleep in the back of my truck. That was it. I placed a phone call to his father. I explained the events of the day and asked if it were possible for him to come and get Jerry. He agreed, but it would be a couple of hours before he could get there. "Fine," I said.

Jerry's dad arrived around ten o'clock, and we went straight to my truck to get Jerry.

The truck was empty!

We called all the adults and boys together and searched the area. There was no sign of Jerry. We looked for a full two hours, but nothing. Finally, I placed a call to the Park Ranger's office and explained our situation. They told us they would take care of everything from hereon, and for us to return to our camp. We did, but nobody went to sleep. We stayed around the campfire, waiting for Jerry to come back.

Dawn had barely broken, when the ranger's jeep pulled into camp. The ranger took Mr. Martin and myself to the side. They'd found Jerry -- he was dead. They had found him about a mile and a half from the campsite . . . over in the National Cemetery. We jumped into the jeep and the ranger took us there.

Jerry's body was in a section of the cemetery set aside for unknown Confederate soldiers. It was sprawled across a stone marker, number 186. His father was in tears as he made the identification. They took the body to town for an autopsy, but the doctors were unable to determine the cause of death.

It was a very sad funeral. All Jerry's friends were on hand to pay their respects.

I went over to Jerry's house after it was over -- partly to console the family, and partly to relieve some of my guilt feelings. It felt strange to be in Jerry's house, and to see all that Civil War stuff . . . the flags and pictures and all. One picture, in particular, caught my eye. It appeared to be an old picture of Jerry in a Confederate uniform. The picture looked so authentic. I asked his dad how they had aged it.

"Oh, that's not Jerry," he replied. "That's one of my ancestors -- a Virginia boy. We don't know too much about him. He ran off to join the war -- even lied about his age. He was only fourteen. His family received one letter containing this picture, and never heard from him again. Does look a lot like Jerry, though, doesn't it?"

I quietly nodded and left the house.

Now, things were beginning to make sense. Maybe Jerry was possessed -- possessed by the spirit of an ancestor who had died long ago, an ancestor who was reaching from beyond the grave to tell his family about his final hours. Through Jerry, it was obvious that the young boy in that picture had experienced tremendous fear in the days preceding his first big battle. He probably sat in the woods for hours, listening to the noise of Union cannonballs crashing around him -- maybe even covered his ears with his hands. He heard the blaring of bugles and charged up the hill, as Union bullets whistled by. Then came the clashing of metal, as bayonets touched in hand-to-hand fighting. Finally, he experienced the pain -- sharp excruciating pain -- as his side was pierced by a Union saber on Cemetery Ridge. From there, he most likely was taken to a field hospital -- a tent -- where he died, leaving no identification, no papers. His body was placed with all the other unknown Confederate soldiers, and subsequently buried beneath stone marker 186.

Was it really Jerry who died at Gettysburg? Or did an ancestor return from the war to disclose his final resting place?

We'll never know!

A NIGHT AT THE DELANEY HOUSE

"I can't believe we're really doing this," Jerry exclaimed, as he quietly opened the window and climbed in. "We're actually going to spend the night at the Delaney place."

"You bet we are," answered Tom. Remember the Scout Law -- "A SCOUT IS BRAVE."

Brian Winkler was the town bully. He always wore this black leather jacket with an eagle on the back -- as if he were trying to impress someone. Coming from a broken home, he pretty much did as he pleased. He constantly cut school and, as a result, was two grades behind for his age. The teachers didn't seem to mind him playing hooky, because when he was at school, he was a distraction to the other students. Brian liked to pick on younger boys, teasing and taunting them. He constantly rode Jerry and Tom, in particular, because they were "Scouts," and Scouts were a bunch of sissies, as far as Brian was concerned.

"Yeah. We'll show Brian we're not afraid," echoed Jerry, as he took the remaining supplies from Tom and placed them on the floor. There was a flashlight, some candles, matches, and a deck of cards to pass the time.

Within a minute, Tom climbed through the window and quickly closed it behind him. They had made it!

"This place gives me the creeps," Jerry whispered. "Do you think all those stories are true?"

The house had been built about 50 years ago by Mr. Edward Delaney in preparation for his marriage to Eleanor Bartholomew. He worked on the house night and day for almost a year, paying attention to every little detail. The house was completed only two days before the wedding. Even after the marriage, Edward Delaney spent much of his time putting the finishing details on the house. Not so much, however, that he didn't find time to father a son, Michael Andrew. This new addition to the family changed Edward Delaney's life. He began to spend more time with his wife and child than he did with the house. Then it happened. One night Edward Delaney, for no apparent reason, slipped into his son's bedroom and, as the boy slept, killed him with an axe. He returned to his bedroom and repeated this ghastly act on his wife. Then, Edward Delaney went to his desk and wrote a little note, before putting a pistol to his head and taking his life. When the police arrived, they found the three bodies and the note. In it, Edward explained that the house had made him kill his family because it was jealous of how he was now spending more time with them than with it. When he realized what he had done, he decided to kill himself. Obviously, the police thought he was crazy. They determined that it was a murder/suicide by a mentally disturbed father. It was several years before someone else moved into the house, a young couple -- the Everettes -- and their baby girl. They were in the house only three months when there was a tragic fire. Nobody knows exactly how it started. Fortunately, the firemen were able to confine the blaze to one upstairs' bedroom. Unfortunately, for some unexplained reason, all three of the Everettes were in that room, and they all perished. A realty company fixed the damage, and again put the house on the market. Several families tried to live there, but none lasted very long. They complained of hearing strange noises at night and some even said they saw ghosts. People believed the house was haunted. The last family to live there was the Oswalds, and that was twenty years ago. Mrs. Oswald came home one night to find her husband hanging from the ceiling. She went raving mad. When the police found her, she was trying to spread gasoline around the house in an attempt to burn it down. They had to have her committed. Since then, nobody has lived there. Even much of the old furniture remains.

"Nah," said Tom. "They're just stories. I bet Brian Winkler made them up."

The boys began to check out the house.

"If my mom and dad knew what I was doing, they'd kill me."

"Yeah. Mine, too."

"I still don't believe how well our plan worked. My mom thinks I'm spending the night next door at your house." "And mine thinks I'm over at yours. You can't beat that for planning."

The rooms were dusty and sheets covered most of the old furniture, but, except for that, the house was in pretty good shape for all its disuse. Tom's flashlight shown on a picture of a man, hanging on the wall ahead.

"Mr. Delaney, I guess."

"Tom! Those eyes are following us!" yelled Jerry.

"Just a reflection. Calm down. Where shall we spend the night?"

"Upstairs, in the 'death room.' That's where we told Brian we'd stay."

"Are you sure, Jerry?"

"Well, I sure don't want to spend the night down here with that creepy old picture looking at me all night."

The boys carried their gear up the stairs and into the large room at the top. It was a bedroom. There was a huge bed, some dressers, and a small table with two chairs. Jerry took the sheets off the table and chairs and threw them in the corner.

Meanwhile, Tom took a candle, placed it on the table and lit it. They decided to play cards to pass the time.

"This was probably the room where Mrs. Delaney was axed," Jerry stated.

"Shut up."

"And where the Everettes were burned to death."

"Just stories, Jerry. Be quiet."

"What time do you have?"

"Ten o'clock. It'll be morning before we know it. Won't Brian be surprised?"

"Yeah. No more 'Scouts are sissies'."

The two boys continued to play cards.

"What time is it now, Tom?"

"Ten minutes later than the last time you asked me. It's almost midnight."

Suddenly the boys began to feel cold. The temperature in the room was falling fast.

"I don't like this," Jerry said. Tom could see Jerry's breath as he spoke.

The candle started to flicker. Tom barely had time to grab the flashlight before the candle went out.

The two boys had had enough. They grabbed their stuff and started to run for the door, but before they got two feet, a wall of flames blocked their way. The reddish glow was frightening. They retreated toward the corner of the room. The flames were slowly making their way toward them.

"Listen!" Tom cried at Jerry.

Jerry listened. Above the roar of the fire he could hear it: "DIE! DIE! DIE!"

Tom and Jerry pondered their next move. The fire was still inching its way across the room.

"Let's make for the window!"

"Okay."

They were off in a flash. Suddenly, Tom grabbed Jerry and both came to an abrupt stop. There above the window, in the red glow of the fire, hung a noose -- a hangman's noose. Both boys retreated.

Maybe it was their imagination, but the cry, "DIE! DIE! DIE!" seemed to be getting louder.

They were getting desperate.

"Look -- that fire!" Jerry screamed. "It's there, but it's not consuming anything. I don't think it's real!"

"I don't know I can feel the heat!"

Suddenly, the sheets which Jerry had thrown in the corner began to rise and take ghostly shapes. The red glow of the fire made them look even more threatening. Fire or no fire, the boys ran for the door.

Jerry was right Both boys went through the flames. They weren't real. They ran out the door, down the stairs, and out the front door of the house. They never saw the dark-haired teenager in the black leather jacket on the bottom floor, yelling "DIE! DIE! DIE!"

'What chickens! They don't look like brave Scouts to me,' thought Brian Winkler from his hiding place.

Tom and Jerry didn't stop running until they were home. Each told his parents that he was sick. It was an excuse that they had agreed upon as they were running home . . . and it was believable. Both boys were very pale.

It was almost noon when Jerry got out of bed. He got dressed, went downstairs, and ate breakfast -- or maybe it was lunch. Shortly after that, there was a knock on the door. It was Tom.

"How'd it go?"

"Fine. How about you?"

"Great, my parents believed everything."

Just then, Jerry's mother entered the room from outside, where she had been talking with neighbors. She had a shocked look on her face.

"What's the matter, mom?" Jerry asked.

"It's horrible. Early this morning the police found the body of a boy, not much older than you two, in the Delaney house. Someone by the name of Brian Winkler. Evidently, he hung himself sometime last night."

The two boys stared at each other, both knowing that the house had struck again.

THEY
NEVER
SURRENDERED

When one thinks of war-like Indians, one always thinks of the Apaches and the Sioux. These are two of the fiercest and most well known of the Indian tribes. Geronimo and his Apache braves terrorized the southwest United States for many years. Sitting Bull, Crazy Horse, and their Sioux warriors annihilated General Custer at the battle of Little Big Horn.

Did you know, though, that not all the Indian wars of the nineteenth century took place in the Arizona desert or in the Black Hills of South Dakota.

Brian Evans didn't, but many years ago he found out in the strangest of ways.

Brian was on a camping trip with his parents at the Everglades National Park in southern Florida. It was summer vacation and Brian was having a great time swimming and fishing. Brian's home was in Maryland and this was a pleasant change. Everything was so different.

Late one afternoon Brian decided to go on a hike to explore the area around the campsite. Like most boys, he was very adventurous. He had been walking for about an hour when a big splash in the nearby swamp startled him.

It was a little alligator. Brian peeked at it from behind a small bush. The alligator swam in the water until it was joined by a larger one.

"Probably its mother or father," Brian thought. "Boy, this is exciting. I can't wait to tell my friends in Maryland."

He would like to have watched some more, but, unfortunately, it was time to start back. He had been gone a long time and his parents would be worried if he didn't return soon. As Brian moved along the trail, it started to get dark. Night was still hours away, but the angle of the sun and the thickness of the trees cast eerie shadows on the path. Brian moved more quickly.

Suddenly, he began to hear noises -- as if someone were following him. His quick pace turned into a run. Brian was scared. Whatever was behind him was gaining. He could hear the sounds of footsteps and breaking twigs getting closer. Brian was so rapt in what was behind him that he didn't notice the large shadowy figure blocking the trail ahead. He ran right into its waiting arms.

Brian looked up to see his captor. It was an Indian. It didn't have feathers or war paint, but Brian knew. He could tell by the darkened skin, the long black hair set back with a headband, and the breech cloth. He was an Indian, all right. This large Indian quickly was joined by three other Indians. Brian had been right. He was being followed.

The Indians grabbed Brian and took him into the woods. It was now almost totally dark, but the Indians needed no light. They moved quietly and quickly through the swamp. Sometimes they walked on the trails and sometimes in the water itself. It was truly amazing how they found their way. Brian was exhausted. It seemed like they had walked forever when, suddenly, they came upon a small clearing with a fire. Brian could see by the dim light of the fire that there were several small huts in the clearing -- and several more Indians.

'This must be their camp,' he thought.

As they entered the village, something else caught Brian's eye. Over in the corner of the clearing was an odd-shaped cypress tree, and sitting at its base was a man. He was wearing the uniform of a cavalry officer. Brian had seen many like it on television and in the movies. But what was he doing here? His hands obviously were tied to the tree. He wasn't moving.

The Indians put Brian in a small thatched hut and tied his hands and feet. He was very scared. None of this made any sense. He wondered what the Indians had in store for him. It wasn't long before he got an idea.

The screams of the cavalry officer sounded in the distance. They were intermittent, and mixed with the laughter of the Indians. Obviously, the Indians were torturing him. How, Brian didn't know, and he really didn't want to. He tugged frantically at his ropes.

Brian jumped as someone came running into the hut. He expected he was next. He turned to see an Indian squaw with her knife drawn. This was it. Brian started to scream. In one swift movement, the squaw put her hand over Brian's mouth and motioned for him to be quiet. She took the knife and cut the ropes from his hands and feet. Then, with her hand, she pointed toward the door.

Funny, that's just what Brian had in mind, too.

It was too late. Before Brian could make his move, another Indian entered the hut. It was one of the braves who had brought Brian to the village. When he saw Brian loose, he ran toward him. Suddenly, the Indian froze and let out a scream. His body staggered and he fell to the earth with a thud. The knife that the squaw had used to cut Brian free was stuck in his back. Again, the squaw motioned toward the door. Brian was gone in a flash.

The scream had alerted the other Indians. They all were running toward the hut. The squaw tried to stop them, but they were too strong and too many. She did manage to buy Brian some time with her efforts, but finally was subdued with a tomahawk blow to the head. When Brian saw this, he knew he was on his own. He ran as fast as his young feet would carry him.

As Brian ran down the trail he could hear the Indians gathering their gear for the chase. They were in no hurry. They knew the swamp like nobody else. No mere boy could escape them. Brian was determined to give it a good try.

Brian had been running for thirty minutes, but it seemed like thirty hours. He could hear the sounds of the Indians in the bushes to his rear. How long would it be before they caught up? He kept running.

Then he heard the yells. They were coming from the other direction -- from in front of him. "Brian, Brian," they echoed through the woods. 'It must be his parents or some rescuers,' he thought. He'd been gone a very long time. He ran toward them.

The race was on. Brian could hear the sounds of the Indians gaining on him from the rear and the yells of his rescuers to the front. Who would reach him first? He continued to run.

Then Brian felt the pain as something came crashing into his head. The warm blood flowing from the wound covered his face. He collapsed to the ground.

The next thing Brian remembered was being shaken awake. He opened his groggy eyes and screamed.

"It's okay, Brian," the voice answered. "We're with the Park Service. You're all right now. We'll take you to your parents. They've been looking for you. First, we'll bandage that nasty gash on your head."

Back at the campsite, Brian was reunited with his parents. He told them and the Park Service Rangers about the Indians. They were all very amused.

"Must have been a dream caused by the hit on the head, or the exhaustion," they remarked. There was no convincing them, so Brian gave up trying.

As Brian grew up, his parents often kidded him about his 'adventure', but he never took it as a joke. Brian knew it was real. This was the main reason he took up archeology as a profession and chose to specialize in American Indians. He would prove them wrong.

He learned the history of all the Indian tribes, their artifacts and customs. In particular, he learned about the

Seminoles, the only Indians native to Florida.

During the Great Seminole Wars of 1835, a band of warriors, led by Osceola, masterminded a highly effective program of harassment against the U.S. Army in the large, eerie swampland of southern Florida. The Seminoles hid men, women, and children in the depths of the everglades, safe from vengeance, and carried on their rebellion with skill and daring. From hiding, they emerged to strike such strongholds as Fort Drane and Micanopy. Once, Major Dade, a U.S. Army officer, took a detachment of men into the swamp to attack the Indians. He was cut off and only two or three of his men escaped. Many were killed or captured. It was impossible to attack villages that could not be found. It was mainly through treachery that Osceola was captured in 1837, only to die a year later. His death increased the Seminole's desire to remain free, and the war continued until 1842. Many Indians chose to remain in the swamps and maintain the struggle, rather than surrender to the white man. Peace was not officially signed until 1926, and even then there were rumors of Indians in the swamp who would not surrender.

It was 1987 when Brian returned to the everglades. Under the guise of looking for Indian artifacts, he had his first chance to look for that lost Indian village. After weeks of searching, his expedition came upon a clearing deep in the swamp. The lay of the land indicated that it would have been ideal for an Indian encampment. As they approached the clearing, Brian saw it . . . the cypress tree. He would have recognized it anywhere. This was the place!

Sure enough, it was a major archeological find. The expedition found many Indian artifacts, proving Seminoles once inhabited the camp. They also discovered several grave sites near the clearing. Very carefully, they unearthed the bodies.

They say that dead men tell no tales, but that's not true. Much can be learned from the dead. Several bodies apparently were Army officers. One could tell from the facial bone-structure that they weren't Indians, and several U.S. Army buttons and buckles were found nearby. There also was a male Indian who, from the notched bones, apparently had died from a sharp object, most likely a knife, which had been thrust in his back. Then, there was a female Indian who had died from a blow to the head. Her skull was fractured.

Brian was ecstatic. This confirmed the events of his youth. Now only one test remained to prove his story. He sent the bones and other objects to the laboratory to be dated.

'What a find,' he thought, 'proof that Seminoles existed in the swamp twenty years ago.' It had to be. Everything was there, just like he remembered.

Brian couldn't wait to open the report the day it arrived from the lab.

"It can't be," he said, dropping the envelope to the floor. They say the bones are approximately 150 years old -- but I saw those Indians when I was a boy, only twenty years ago. I did. I tell you.

Did Brian really see the Indians? Or had he been dreaming?

Research has showed that there have been other campers who have gotten lost in the everglades -- lost without a trace. Were they the victims of the swamp and its quicksand and alligators -- or were they the victims of a group of Seminole Indians who refused to surrender? Indians who continue to battle the white man -- even beyond death.

ADVENTURE ALONG THE CANAL

The Chesapeake and Ohio Canal, more commonly known as the C&O Canal, was a major engineering undertaking for its time. Started in 1828, it was designed to connect the rich Eastern seaboard with the unlimited raw materials of the west. Beginning at Washington, D.C., it would parallel the Potomac River and eventually extend to Cumberland, Maryland -- a distance of 185 miles. However, by its completion in 1850, it already was obsolete, the B&O Railroad having reached there eight years earlier. Still, the C&O Canal managed to serve the area well for 72 years before its closing in 1922.

The canal is not without its share of stories, many documented in history. For instance, the Civil War almost ended at Williamsport, when General Robert E. Lee, fleeing from Gettysburg, could not cross the rain-swollen Potomac River. Also, John Brown hid in a farmhouse near the canal until one rainy night in October, 1859, when he crossed into Harper's Ferry. There he attacked the United States Arsenal.

The following story has not been documented in history books, but has been passed by word of mouth from generation to generation along the canal. It's the story of Big Red, the Irishman.

In the early days when the canal was being built, there were at times over 6000 laborers using pick-axes and stump pullers working along the canal. Many of these men were German and Irish emigrants, drawn to the canal because of the high pay -- $10.00 a month -- and meat and whiskey every day. Unfortunately, things did not always turn out as promised. The work was hard and demanding. The Irish and the Germans often fought and rioted because of non-payment of wages. When they weren't fighting management, they fought among themselves. Such was life along the canal.

Several hundred men were assigned to work on the Paw Paw Tunnel section of the canal. Here, the Potomac River underwent a six mile bend that required a tunnel, nearly a mile long, be blasted through the mountain. The hardest work was assigned to two crews, one German and one Irish. These two crews worked continuously on the tunnel, using pick-axes, shovels, and blasting powder. From the start, the project was slow. The Irish and the Germans never got along. The Germans accused the Irish of not doing their share of the work. All day long they would taunt the Irish laborers. Everyone knew that one day something bad would happen. Finally, it did.

On the way back to their camp after work, a small group of Germans was confronted by several Irish workers carrying clubs. The Irish were led by a giant of a man with red hair, known as Big Red. He chided the Germans.

"So you think we don't do enough of the work. We'll show you what we can do."

With those words, the Irish attacked the Germans. The fight lasted only a few minutes and the outnumbered Germans took a beating. They dragged their wounded back to camp.

Everything appeared normal at work the next day. Both the Germans and the Irish kept to themselves. The Germans, however, were just biding their time. A plan was already being made for revenge. They were waiting for the right time.

The time came Friday night. Big Red was summoned from camp to the supervisor's cabin, located about a half mile away. The Germans waited in ambush. Without notice, they sprang upon him. Big Red put up a struggle, but eventually was overcome.

"Kill him!" the leader of the Germans instructed, "but make it look like an accident."

Big Red spit and cursed.

"An accident!" he shouted; "this deed will not go un-avenged. You and all your kind, be plagued with acci-dents!"

Before he could say another word, a club fell upon his head, and he was dead. Before returning to camp, the Germans tossed Big Red's body from a nearby cliff where it was discovered the next morning. From all appearances, it looked as if he had fallen from the cliff in the dark. His body was taken to the worker's cemetery, located on the canal, near Purslane Run, and buried.

Hardly any of the Irish really believed that Big red had been killed by an accident, but they had no proof. They knew that somehow the Germans were involved. Eventually they would find out how. It all became irrelevant. That afternoon, as the Germans were working on the tunnel, a blasting charge went off early. The Germans had not had time to clear the area and were trapped by the falling rock. Many were left dead and dying.

The Irish thought this was an act of God to avenge Big Red's death. The Germans knew it was the revenge of Big Red himself.

The tunnel explosion was just the first of many accidents that began to plague the workers -- and the strangest thing was that most of the accidents involved Germans.

Was this a coincidence? The Germans didn't think so.

It was rumored that, at times, Big Red could be seen wandering through the dark chambers of the tunnel. But that couldn't be so. He was dead! The accidents continued. Many Germans who were involved in Big Red's murder remembered his curse and left the canal to look for new work. As the number of German workers decreased, so did the number of accidents. Still, a tunnel that was estimated to take three years to build, took twenty-two.

In 1850, the C&O Canal was finished -- but not the accidents. They continued. At Lock 27, near Spink's Ferry, a German boatman fell from his barge and was crushed against the side of the canal. Years later, a German crewman mysteriously disappeared from his boat one night. His body was found floating in the canal the next morning. Every so often, there were reports of a big man with red hair stalking the trail. So it was for the life of the canal. Strange accidents kept occurring, usually involving a German.

The canal was closed in 1922. Everyone thought that this would bring an end to the haunting of Big Red and the tragic accidents, but it was not to be. One day as a group of workers was clearing the trail near a cliff, they were pelted by falling rocks. Only one worker was seriously hurt -- a German! His skull had been fractured. He died on the way to the hospital.

Even women and children were not safe from Big Red's curse. Once, a woman jogger tripped for no reason at all and broke her leg. While waiting for assistance, she reported seeing a man with red hair peering out from the bushes. Then, an eleven-year-old boy, camping at a hiker-biker campsite along the canal, was killed by a tree that fell for no apparent reason. Both were of German descent.

The accidents continued until 1972 when a Boy Scout troop was taking a hike along the canal tow path. The canal was in very bad shape due to Hurricane Agnes which had caused several million dollars worth of damage to the canal two months earlier. Many sections of the tow path were completely washed away.

As the Scouts walked down the trail, little did they know that the next "accident" was about to happen. Big Red was watching . . . waiting . . . waiting for the right place and time. He already had selected the victim -- Karl Kreuger, a twelve-year-old boy. One look at his blond hair and blue eyes indicated he was German. It was just a matter of time.

During a rest, several boys, including Karl, left the trail to get a closer look at the river. The Potomac, normally a slow moving river, was flowing fast and turbulent due to the hurricane weeks earlier. The river banks were muddy and covered with debris.

Big Red got poised. The time for the "accident" was growing near.

Suddenly, however, before Big Red could act, there was a loud crash as a section of the river bank collapsed into the raging river, taking a Scout with it. The swift waters swept the boy away.

"It's Al!" yelled Karl. "Go for help!"

Al Kelly, whose great grandparents were from Ireland, was a small boy and could not swim very well.

Karl reacted quickly, kicking off his shoes and jumping into the river to save Al. With considerable effort he was able to reach him and bring him to shore. The other Scouts were pulling Al to safety when Karl lost his balance and fell back into the raging river. He was gone in a flash. With no more energy left, he was pulled under. Several Scouts jumped in trying to locate him, but couldn't. Karl was gone.

They searched the water and shore for twenty minutes, but found nothing. Everyone had given up hope when they located Karl several hundred yards downstream, sitting beside a tree. He was tired, wet, and scared, but except for that, he was fine.

He told everyone that he was going under the water when he felt this big hand grab him and pull him to the surface.

"It was a big man with red hair. He pulled me over to shore and laid me against this tree. I must have blacked out for a second," Karl continued, "because when I turned around he was gone."

Since then, the accidents have ceased. Usage of the canal has increased considerably. Hikers, bikers, and joggers no longer travel the canal in fear -- particularly if they're German. They no longer keep an eye peeled for that big man with red hair who may be stalking them along the trail. And they owe it all to Karl, a German boy, who was willing to sacrifice his life to save that of an Irish friend ... thus undoing a wrong of over a century before.

At last, Big Red was at peace.

DON'T GO TO BURNING ISLAND

They really had no intention of going to Burning Island. They were just out for a weekend away from it all -- away from the hustle-bustle of college life. But the warning of the old man down at the dock remained in their ears.

"Don't go to Burning Island," he warned, "that place is evil. It's haunted!"

Until that moment, Joe, Wayne, Chris, and Harold never had heard of the place. They prodded the old man to tell the tale. So he did.

"Over a hundred years ago, Indians lived on this little island in the middle of the river. They lived a very peaceful life, fishing and hunting. Then one day it happened -- no one knows exactly how -- but there was a big fire. It took place in the middle of the night and caught the Indians by surprise. The fire spread fast. It destroyed their wooden canoes, cutting off their only escape. The flames could be seen for miles. When help arrived from town, it was too late. The entire tribe had been wiped out -- burned to death -- men, women and children. It was not a pretty sight. They buried the charred remains of the Indians in a mass grave-yard on the island. They renamed the dreary-looking island

with all its charred trees 'Burning Island', and so it has remained until this day. Over the years vegetation returned and the island became a pretty place again, but no one ever settled there. It's not that no one tried. At least twice in recent times, people have tried, but they never lasted more than a few days. They said Indians haunted the place. No one else tried. To this day, Burning Island remains a place to be avoided by everyone."

As they canoed, the boys joked about the old man's warning. "Don't go to Burning Island," they would yell at each other and laugh. But the more they joked, the more intriguing Burning Island got. Weren't they looking for a place to get away from it all? A place where they wouldn't be bothered. A place where they could "do their thing" without interference. Burning Island was the ideal place. Nobody went there. Besides, it would be an adventure. Their classmates would envy their courage for spending the night on Burning Island.

"Don't go to Burning Island! Bah. Burning Island, here we come."

Chris had the map of the area and, sure enough, Burning Island was there. It was about six miles downstream from where they were. They paddled and paddled. The boys could hardly wait for the adventure that lay ahead. With each stroke, they thought of the activities they had planned for that evening. They had looked forward to this weekend for a long time . . . and here it was. Now, in addition, they had the extra excitement of Burning Island and its Indian ghosts. Wow!

The canoes pulled up to Burning Island late in the afternoon. The old man was right about one thing. It was a beautiful place. They dragged the canoes on shore and unloaded the gear. They placed the paddles against a tree near the canoes.

After scouting the area, the boys decided to set up camp in a clearing about a hundred yards away from the canoes. It was a good spot. It was located among the trees with plenty of room for the two tents and a fire. They pitched camp and stored the gear in a matter of minutes. Chris and Wayne gathered firewood while Harold and Joe began to prepare supper. This trip was everything they had thought it would be, and more. It was a lot better than life in the dorm.

After supper, darkness set in, but the boys kept the fire burning bright. This was the time they were waiting for. Time to sit back and relax and to "do their thing." They popped open a few cans of beer and Wayne took the little plastic bag from his pack.

As they drank and smoked, they talked about college life and other things. They laughed about the old man and his warning "Don't go to Burning Island." After all, this was what the weekend was about -- having fun. By eleven o'clock, they still were sitting around the fire talking, glassy-eyed.

Chris was the first to notice it. As he stared into the fire, the smoke began to take the shape of Indians rising into the night. The others laughed when he told them about it, but, within minutes, they, too, began to see the

shapes. The forms unmistakably were those of Indians --
Indians on fire -- howling and screaming. They stared in
amazement at the transformations. The smoke forms
looked so real, so life-like.

Without warning, the Indian forms leaped from the
fire at the boys. Harold never got off his feet. Two Indians
were upon him in an instant. The cigarette fell from his
lips and he dropped his can of beer. He was powerless to
get the Indians off of him -- to get those hands from around
his throat.

The flames had spread from the campfire to the woods.
The whole island appeared to be on fire. There were
Indians everywhere.

The other boys had managed to get to their feet and
were making a valiant effort to run for the canoes. Joe and
Wayne were in the front, about twenty feet ahead of Chris.
They ran as fast as they could. Joe and Wayne stopped
when they heard the scream. It was Chris. They turned.
In the red glow of the burning trees they could see an
Indian pulling a knife from Chris' stomach. They watched,
helpless, as their friend's body fell to the ground.

They again ran for the canoes. They raced the Indians
and the fire. Flames jumped out at them from all sides.
This was the longest hundred yards they had run in their
lives. Finally, they reached the canoes. Quickly, they
began to push one of them out into the water when suddenly Wayne froze.

"The paddles," he screamed, "they're over near the
trees!"

He dropped the canoe and ran for the woods, barely thirty feet away.

Wayne had the paddles in his hand when he heard it. It was a loud screeching war-whoop. Wayne turned and saw this huge Indian holding a large rock in his hands above his head. The rock came crashing down on Wayne's skull.

Joe could wait no longer. The whole island was on fire. He could hear the screams of the Indians coming closer. The shadows seemed to move in the red glow. He could no longer see Wayne, and Wayne did not respond to his calls.

Suddenly, three Indians charged from the woods. Joe took his knife from the holder on his belt and threw it. It passed right through them. That was it. Paddles or no paddles, he pushed the canoe into the water. As he drifted away, he looked back to see the entire island engulfed in flames. Indians were dancing on the beach, as if in victory. He collapsed in the boat.

Some fishermen found Joe the next morning. He was delirious. He kept repeating, "Don't go to Burning Island." He kept muttering nonsense about Indians and the murder of his friends. It was obvious he was mad. The fishermen took Joe on board and towed the canoe to town. Once there, Joe was turned over to the authorities. They took him to the hospital and listened to his story. It was unreal. It just couldn't be true. Regardless, they had to investigate. They organized a search party and set out in their boats for Burning Island.

As the search party neared the island, there were no signs of any fire. The trees and shrubs were as green and beautiful as ever. On the east side, they could see a canoe pulled neatly up on the shore. They docked their boats and went about the search.

Not far from the canoe, they found the body of a boy. It was Wayne. His head had been bashed in. Nearby, on the ground, lay a large blood-covered rock. Fifty yards up the trail, they found another body. It was Chris. There was a large wound in his belly where he had been stabbed by some sharp instrument. There was no knife or other object found. The searchers were greatly disturbed.

"What possibly could have happened on this small island?"

Shortly after, they came upon the campsite . . . and in the middle of the campsite, near a campfire that had long burned out, they found Harold. His face was frozen in fear. The marks around his neck indicated he had been strangled.

"What or who could have done such a thing?"

They searched for clues. The campsite was in complete disarray. The tents had been knocked down and torn to shreds. Gear had been thrown all over the place. This was definitely the work of a mad man. Near the campfire, they found a large quantity of empty beer cans, and a little plastic bag -- filled with marijuana.

Now things were beginning to make sense. Obviously, Joe had freaked out on the booze and the drugs, and, in a wild rampage, killed his friends. After all, wasn't there a knife missing from his belt? They took pictures and gathered the evidence, bagged the bodies, and brought everything back to town.

In spite of the evidence, the authorities never prosecuted Joe.

What good would it have done?

Joe was in no shape to undergo a trial. Since he was found in that canoe, he has been confined to the County Mental Hospital. To this day he has maintained his innocence and walks the halls mumbling about Indians.

And now and then he screams: "Don't go to Burning Island!"

AN EAGLE FOR EDDIE

I never thought that Arnold would join Boy Scouts. He was such a fragile little boy. Although eleven years old, he was very small for his age, and obviously had been pampered and spoiled all his life. He never was allowed to play sports. "Arnold might get hurt," his mother would say. And he never had been camping. The woods are full of animals and bugs, and poison ivy, and -- his mom had a million excuses. So, I was surprised when, on my urging, his mother let him visit our Scout meeting one evening. I was even more surprised when she let him join the troop and go on his first campout.

It was a disaster. Rain fell from the time we left Friday evening till the time we got back Sunday afternoon. Actually, *rain* isn't the right word. It poured! I had never seen it rain so hard in all my days as a Scoutmaster. Arnold's tent leaked -- his sleeping bag got soaked -- and he was pretty wet and miserable. He was having a genuine lousy time. If it hadn't have been for Eddie, I doubt if we ever would have seen Arnold on a campout again -- or even at a troop meeting for that matter.

Eddie was an older Scout in the troop. He was fourteen years old and very mature for his age. He had been in the troop for over three years and was an excellent

Scout. Not only did he have knowledge of Scouting skills, but an uncanny ability to get along with other boys. He had attained the rank of Star and was working very diligently up the advancement trail toward Eagle, Scouting's highest award.

Eddie observed all the little problems that Arnold was having on the campout, and took him under his wing. He shared his dry sleeping bag -- helped Arnold to get a fire going -- and showed him wet weather skills. With Eddie's help, Arnold survived.

After the campout was over, Eddie asked me if he could work with Arnold, as sort of a "big brother." He'd take care of him and teach him how to be a good Scout. I agreed. Arnold was going to need all the help he could. Besides, Eddie had all of the necessary skills. He was Eagle Scout material if I ever had seen any . . . and I had seen a few Eagles in my time. It was just a matter of time before he earned the badge.

Eddie prided himself in knowing his Scouting skills. He could do everything, but his specialty was knot tying. He knew his knots so well that every time someone asked him to tie a bowline, he would tie a bowline on a bight to show off. I wondered if Eddie really remembered how to tie a regular bowline anymore.

That's how Arnold and Eddie became friends and started working together. Eddie always gave Arnold extra attention at our weekly troop meetings, and on campouts they were inseparable. They shared the same tent and did most everything together . . . and the results were showing.

Arnold was coming along -- slowly, but surely. With Eddie's help, Arnold made it to Tenderfoot, about the same time Eddie earned his Life badge.

Then it happened. Two days after his fifteenth birthday Eddie collapsed on his way home from school. A neighbor called an ambulance and it rushed Eddie to the hospital. After a series of tests, the doctors determined that he had a rare blood disease. It was incurable. Eddie only had a few weeks to live.

Nobody could believe it. Eddie was so athletic, so healthy. He had never been sick a day in his life. Why him? He had everything to live for.

Arnold visited the hospital almost every day. He would stop on his way home from school and remain until his mother picked him up. He stuck by Eddie the way Eddie had stuck by him on that first campout. Eddie was not a quitter. He fought to the end, but there was nothing he, nor anyone else, could do. He was getting very weak. I was there the night he died. So was Arnold and Eddie's parents. It was very sad.

Eddie's last words to Arnold were for him to stay in Boy Scouts. Arnold said he was scared, but Eddie assured him that he would be there to help.

"Scout's promise," Eddie said.

He made Arnold promise to earn the Eagle Badge that he cherished so much, but now would never get. Arnold cried as he swore he'd do it. Eddie was gone within minutes. We all sat there and cried.

I half-expected never to see Arnold at Scouts again,

but the following Wednesday night he was there. He said he had a promise to keep. He also was on the next campout at Cedarville State Park. I knew the first campout without Eddie would be a critical time for Arnold and I assigned another older boy to look after him, but Arnold objected.

"Eddie will look after me," he said. "Eddie promised."

I backed down, not wanting to get Arnold upset. Arnold spent much of the weekend alone. Other than eating and participating in scheduled group activities, he kept to himself. He even slept alone in his tent. Some boys mentioned that they had seen him walking alone in the woods, talking, but nobody was there. In general, he did very well. There were no complaints and he seemed happy on the trip back home.

Arnold continued to improve his Scouting skills in the months to come. He still was very much of a loner, but was doing well, learning his Scouting skills and advancement. He made his Second Class rank, a feat I would have thought impossible a few months before.

Arnold continued to attend troop meetings and campouts. He never missed a one. He became one of the most active boys in the troop. It was almost as if he had something to prove. I told him how surprised I was that he was doing so well. He looked at me and smiled and said, "Eddie's helping me."

It was the backpack hike in May when Arnold next mentioned Eddie. Backpack hikes usually separate the men from the boys. Most of the smaller boys do not do very well. Arnold's pack weighed a ton. I tried to persuade him to leave some things at home, but he insisted that he could make it. I relented, but I'd keep an eye on him.

Arnold spent most of the hike alone, but toward the middle of the group. This was a surprise, because I would have bet my bottom dollar that he would have been behind with the smaller boys. After the hike I complimented Arnold for doing so well.

"Yeah," he said, "Eddie only had to help me a couple of times."

This continued reference to Eddie as if he were real wasn't healthy. I decided to talk to Arnold's mother.

Arnold's mother stated that since Eddie had died, Arnold had spent much time in his room. He'd always say that he was working on his Scouting, though sometimes she swore she could hear him talking. I told her about his continued references to Eddie and we both agreed to work with Arnold to help him through these troubled times.

It was almost a year after Eddie had died when Arnold earned his First Class. I observed the Board of Review. An adult questioned Arnold about knots and asked him to tie a bowline. Arnold proceeded to tie a bowline on a bight.

I didn't have to see any more. Now I was convinced that Eddie was helping Arnold. Most First Class Scouts don't even know what a bowline on a bight is -- not to mention how to tie one. Only one person could have shown Arnold how to tie that knot and that was Eddie.

The bowline on a bight was his specialty.

It was shortly after that Greg joined the troop. Just like Arnold, Greg was a quiet little boy -- another boy who needed Scouting.

On Greg's first campout, Arnold approached me and asked, "Do you mind if I tent with Greg and help him out? He looks like he's going to need it. Besides, Eddie says that I'm ready to be on my own." Of course, I agreed. This was the first time that Arnold wanted to establish a relationship with anyone since Eddie's death. I thought it would be good for Arnold.

We never heard any more from Arnold about Eddie. Oh, we did discuss fond memories and such, but no more talk of Eddie helping out. Arnold truly was on his own.

Eddie must have returned to the grave knowing that his job was done -- and done well. Arnold matured into one of the best Scouts and leaders the troop had ever seen. He no longer was a loner. He got along with everyone, and always took it upon himself to help smaller, less experienced boys.

It was February 10th, when the troop held Arnold's Eagle Award Ceremony at the school. Eddie had been dead for over three years. When I pinned the Eagle Badge on Arnold's chest, I saw a tear come to his eye. Quietly, he turned to the side and whispered, "We did it! We got our Eagle! Thanks."

The Eagle Badge has meaning to every Scout who earns it, but somehow, I think it meant a little more this night.

DYING
FOR
MILK

For the first time in many years I had lost faith in my Scouts. "A Scout is trustworthy," or so the first line of the Scout Law states. Yet every night for the past four days someone had stolen a bottle of milk from the staff refrigerator. Never in all my days as camp director had I had this sort of problem. My staff always had been honest and dependable.

I first noticed the thefts Tuesday morning. It was obvious. Every evening the staff received twelve bottles of milk from the main storeroom. They placed them in the refrigerator in the staff kitchen to be available for the next morning's breakfast. Tuesday, they brought to my attention that there only were eleven bottles in the refrigerator. My initial reaction was that maybe the storeroom only had sent eleven bottles the night before, but a check of the inventory sheet showed that this wasn't so. We had received our twelve bottles.

I decided not to say anything. No sense getting everyone aroused over a bottle of milk. Someone must have gotten thirsty. Besides, it probably was a one-time thing. It wasn't. Wednesday morning, there were again only eleven bottles of milk in the refrigerator where twelve had been the night before. I questioned the kitchen staff, but nobody knew anything -- or, at least, they weren't talking. When the same thing occurred Thursday and Friday mornings, it was time to take action. I couldn't believe that some Scout was stealing milk, especially since there was soda and bug juice in the same refrigerator, but the evidence was overwhelming. Obviously, when the Scout saw how easy it was to get away with stealing the first time, he continued.

I wasn't concerned about the loss of milk. If someone wanted milk, all they had to do was ask. The fact that a Scout would take something without asking, and continue to do so night after night, infuriated me. Someone was dying for milk.

Four days were enough. I called the staff together for a meeting. Without mentioning the disappearance of the milk, I reminded them of the camp rules regarding the kitchen and food.

"Nobody except kitchen workers are allowed in the kitchen," I admonished. "And nobody helps themselves to any food without permission."

I mixed in several other rules in relation to the staff area in general, such as keeping tents straight and no noise after ten o'clock. My object was not to accuse, but to make the milk thief feel guilty, and stop stealing on his own. This always had been an effective ploy in the past.

It wasn't this time. Another bottle of milk was gone Saturday. Was I mad? I had to take a walk in the woods to calm down. It was bad enough that one of my Scouts would steal, but to continue to do so after yesterday's talk was a slap in the face -- a direct confrontation with me. I always had considered every boy on my staff as a friend . . . and now someone couldn't be trusted. I was determined to find out who.

I called another staff meeting. This time I laid it on the line. I told the boys that someone had been stealing milk from the kitchen for the past five days in direct violation of the rules.

"I don't know who it is, but I'm going to find out. And when I do, you're going to be sorry! Whoever it is, doesn't deserve to be a Scout."

I came down pretty hard on the boys, but I wanted to. I meant every word I'd said. The Scouts left the meeting talking among themselves. I was sure this was the end of it. Peer pressure would win out.

Wrong again. Another bottle of milk was missing Sunday morning. I said nothing.

"Someone is doing this just to get you mad," I said to myself. "Don't let him win."

Later that morning, after the staff left the area to attend to their duties around the camp, I went to work. The thief had stolen six bottles of milk and he had to have hidden the empties somewhere. I checked all the trash cans within walking distance, but found nothing. There wasn't a milk bottle to be found. These Scouts are too smart for that. I went back and searched under the tent floor boards. Still nothing. I even wandered into the

woods to look for the bottles. I know Scouts don't litter
... but they're not supposed to steal either. I found two
soda cans, a half-filled bag of potato chips, and a rusty
pocket knife, but no milk bottles. I gave up. That evening
I set a trap.

Trip wires crisscrossed the door to the kitchen, each
connected to a series of tin cans full of rocks. Anybody
trying to enter the kitchen would make enough noise to
wake the camp. The trap was set. All I had to do was lie
in my tent and wait.

At about one o'clock in the morning, I was startled by
the noise as rocks and tin cans came crashing.

"It's the trap!" I yelled, as I jumped to my feet. "I've got
him now!"

I ran to the kitchen door. There, trying to untangle
himself from the ropes and cans, was John Warner, a boy
staff member.

"So, it's you, Johnny."

"Wait," he replied, "I heard a noise and came out to
investigate. I've never taken any milk."

I went and checked the refrigerator. There was a
bottle of milk missing. Johnny couldn't possibly have
taken it. He hadn't entered the kitchen yet. Then who?
And how?

The next day I broke one of my long-standing princi-
ples. I installed a combination lock on the kitchen door.
Never did I think it would be necessary to lock up anything
on a Scout reservation -- particularly in the staff area -- but
I had tried everything else. Only the head cook, to whom

I had given the combination, and I could enter the kitchen after hours. I wouldn't catch the thief, but, at least, I'd end the thefts.

Or so I thought. Again, there were only eleven bottles of milk in the refrigerator come Tuesday morning. I couldn't believe it. First, the kid had eluded my trap the night before, and now, somehow, the thief had by-passed a locked door. I wasn't dealing with an ordinary Scout thief, this kid was a pro.

"Must be a cat burglar in the off season."

I devised another plan for that night.

Right after dark, I counted the twelve bottles of milk in the refrigerator and had the head cook put the lock on the door -- with me inside. I found a comfortable spot in the corner of the kitchen behind a chair. It was out of sight of the door, yet had a good view of the refrigerator. I sat on the floor and prepared to spend the night. No way would the thief elude me now.

It was two o'clock in the morning when I first heard the noise. Unmistakably, it was the turning of the tumblers on a combination lock. I raised my eyes above the chair to see. The door made a creaking sound as it opened and I ducked down so as not to be seen. "I've got to catch the boy red-handed," I thought. "I've got to catch him with the milk."

The next sound I heard was the opening of the refrigerator door. Now I've got him. With flashlight in hand, I jumped from my hiding place. There, not more than ten feet away from my face, was a bottle of milk. It was floating in mid-air toward the door. I stumbled as I tried to run toward it.

"Darn chair," I cussed. As I picked myself up off the floor, I could see the bottle moving swiftly out the door. When I reached the door it was gone. I closed the door and went to my tent. I sat quietly at the breakfast table the next morning. My faith in my fellow Scouts had been restored, but this did nothing to explain the occurrences of the night before. How could locks open by themselves? How could a bottle float through the air? These were questions that I could not begin to answer.

The answers came that afternoon. The Coyote Patrol of Troop 750 was taking a hike along a lightly-traveled dirt road near the camp when a boy thought he heard a baby cry. The patrol followed the faint whines and came upon a green car that obviously had gone off the road and crashed into a tree. The car could not be seen from the roadway. On investigating, they found the driver of the car, a young woman, was dead. She most likely had died on impact -- a fact the autopsy report would later establish as having happened nine days earlier. Also, strapped in the car seat next to her, was a little baby, only months old. It was alive and faintly crying -- and there on the floor were nine empty bottles of milk.

The mother's love for her child was stronger than death.

 # PIRATE ADVENTURE

CLUNK, CLUNK

There it went again. This time Drew was sure he'd heard it. He'd been sitting in his sleeping bag for the past five minutes listening to the noises of the night.

CLUNK, CLUNK

What could it be? It sounds like someone digging . . . but who . . . and why? The Scoutmaster had sent everyone to bed hours ago. Drew was going to find out. He'd never get any sleep wondering about it.

Slowly and quietly, Drew put on his pants and sneakers, so as not to wake up Bobby, his tentmate, who was sleeping a few feet away.

As Drew left the tent, not another Scout was stirring. The moon shone brightly against the white sands of the campsite. Assateague State Park was a good place to camp. The sandy campsites were such a contrast to the usual trees and grass, and its proximity to the ocean offered many activities for the Scouts.

CLUNK, CLUNK

The sound was coming from the woods to the rear of the campsite and away from the beach. Drew took his flashlight and moved silently toward the sound. Barely twenty-five yards from camp, he caught a glimpse of some shadows in a clearing. He turned off his flashlight and crept closer, being careful not to make a sound. From behind a bush, he clearly could make out two figures in the clearing. One was a small man dressed like an old-time sailor with a large gold ring in his ear. He had a shovel in his hand and was digging a hole in the soft earth. The other figure was a large man who was wearing a bandanna on his head. As the man turned, Drew noticed he was wearing a patch on his eye.

"Oh, my gosh! They're pirates," Drew thought.

The man with the ring in his ear stopped digging and with the help of the larger man placed a big chest in the hole.

Without warning, there was a loud "BANG" and the small man fell to the ground. Drew had been concentrating so hard on the chest that he had failed to see the large man pull a gun. Drew froze.

He watched as the large pirate quickly widened the hole and laid the body across the chest. Drew was very quiet for fear that he, too, might suffer the same fate as the sailor.

Then Drew heard it. Someone was coming and was heading straight toward him.

"I'm a goner," he thought.

The sound was getting closer and closer. Drew ducked down and closed his eyes.

"What are you doing here?"

Drew opened his eyes. It was Bobby.

"I was awakened by this clunking sound, and you were gone from the tent, so I came to investigate."

"Shush!" cautioned Drew, pointing to the clearing. Bobby ducked down next to him.

The pirate was placing the last shovel of soil on the pile. Slowly, he looked around and quietly faded into the night.

Drew and Bobby waited a minute to make sure he had left and then went toward the mound of loose soil in the clearing. Using their hands, they were able to clear away most of the soil. First they came to the body of the sailor ... then they found the chest. It was too heavy to lift from the hole, so they opened the lid and shined their flashlights inside it. They hardly could believe their eyes. The chest was full of little gold coins -- gold doubloons. Each boy took one coin and then they closed the chest. "We'll come back and get it in the morning," they agreed.

Next morning, at the first opportunity, Drew and Bobby went back to the clearing with a shovel. This time they dug and dug, but found nothing. Both boys agreed this was the right clearing, but there was nothing -- no body, no chest, no gold coins.

This was weird. No sense telling anyone what they'd seen. Who'd believe it anyway? Drew and Bobby decided to wait until Sunday when they were leaving to tell their Scoutmaster they 'found' some coins.

That night the Park Service had an informative campfire program and the troop attended. The ranger told of the area's history, which included mention of the pirates that used many coves in the area for refuge.

"Rumors have it," he said, "that some pirates even buried their treasure nearby for safekeeping."

Drew and Bobby smiled at each other.

"Sometimes they even killed the people who buried it. This was done for two reasons. First, it left no witnesses. Second, the bodies of the dead were buried with the treasure so their ghosts could protect it."

Drew and Bobby looked at each other again. This time they weren't smiling.

Later that night a scream awakened the Scouts. It was Joey. He said that he had heard something walking around the campsite and when he looked from his tent he'd seen a man.

"It was a pirate," Joey cried, "and he was looking for something."

Everyone laughed.

"No more pirate stories for you, Joey," kidded the Scoutmaster.

"But I did see him," rebuffed Joey. "He had a big gold ring in his ear."

Drew looked pale.

All the Scouts went back to bed, but not all went back to sleep. Drew and Bobby lay awake, listening.

The next morning as Drew and Bobby were packing to leave, Drew said to Bobby, "Go get your coin and we'll tell the Scoutmaster." Bobby ran to his pack where he had hidden the coin. The pack was on its side. There was a big slit cut in the back and the coin was gone. But how was that -- nobody knew it was there? The pirate must have taken it. Bobby ran back and told Drew.

The two boys decided not to tell the Scoutmaster after all. "This is weird," Drew scowled, "I'm glad we're leaving."

"Me, too," added Bobby.

The Scouts loaded all the gear and were ready to leave. Everyone got into the cars and began to drive off. Drew was in Mr. Rodgers' car.

CATHUNK, CATHUNK, CATHUNK

"What's that, Mr. Rodgers?" asked the boys.

"I think we've got a flat tire."

Mr. Rodgers got out and investigated. Sure enough, the right rear tire was flat with a two inch gash in the side.

"Gee, I don't know how that happened. Looks like it was done with a large knife. Okay, Everyone out of the car while I change the tire."

As Mr. Rodgers changed the tire, the boys played tag. All the other cars had left. In fifteen minutes, Mr. Rodgers had changed the tire and was ready to leave again. He summoned the boys. "Be right there," yelled Drew as he headed for the woods. "I've got to go to the bathroom."

As Drew was standing there, relieving himself against a tree, he heard a noise behind him.

"Boy, I'm glad we're leaving," Drew said without turning. There was no answer.

Drew turned, but instead of another Scout like he expected, there stood the pirate with a gold ring in his ear. There was a mean look on his face and he had his hand held out. Without making a sound, Drew reached into his pocket, and shakingly withdrew the coin and placed it in the pirate's hand. Then he ran for the car as fast as he could.

On the ride home, Mr. Rodgers recounted the weekend.

"Another campout full of fun . . . a lot of fun, but no excitement."

'No excitement at all,' Drew thought sarcastically to himself.

TAKE CARE
OF
MOM

Ted and Ned Albright were an oddity in Troop 1250. They were twins. They looked so much alike in their Scout uniforms you couldn't tell them apart. Mr. Adams, their Scoutmaster, made them wear nametags so he could tell the difference. Both were First Class Scouts and hardly had missed an activity in the two years they had been in the troop.

The two were inseparable. They even shared the same room at home where they lived alone with their mother. Their father had died four years previous when they were eight years old. Their mother was very supportive of the Scouting Program because it filled a void in the boys' lives -- at a time when they needed it most.

Thus, it was odd, on the troop's winter campout in January at Catoctin National Park, that only Ted was present. Unfortunately, Ned had come down with a very bad cold. He was running a slight fever, so his mother made him stay home. This was the first time anyone could remember either of the twins doing something on his own. Actually, if Mrs. Albright had had her way, both boys would be home on this brisk January weekend. She always had been an over-protective parent, but even more so the last few years since the death of her husband. It wasn't easy being both mother and father to two boys approaching their teens. But the twins also had done considerable growing up in those four years -- doing their share of the chores and other household responsibilities. They truly were the little men of the house, and Scouting had had a lot to do with it. So Mrs. Albright quietly gave in to Ted when he pleaded for her to let him go camping without Ned.

The Scouts met Friday night. Mrs. Albright made Ted dress in his warmest winter clothes and took him down to meet the other boys. The cars already were there and the Scouts were loading the gear when they arrived. Ted took his gear from the car and loaded it into Mr. Adams' truck, then turned and kissed his mother goodbye.

Saturday started off like a typical January weekend in Maryland -- brisk and cold. Mrs. Albright was worried, but this was nothing new. She would have been worried if this were a summer campout. It was her nature. She often worried about the boys. She worried while she was at work and they were at school . . . and she always worried when they were camping. Maybe she wouldn't have been so worried if it hadn't started snowing.

I have been a Scoutmaster for many years and I often wonder what parents at home think while their sons are camping. I'm sure they usually think the worst, while the boys are having the times of their lives. Boys are a lot tougher than most people think. Parents usually worry for nothing. This time, however, Mrs. Albright would be right.

On the way back from a hike to Camp David, the president's retreat, located a few miles from Catoctin, the snow turned to sleet. By the time the Scouts had arrived back at their campsite, the sleet had turned to rain -- ice cold, wet rain. There's no worse weather for winter camping. Snow is tolerable, even enjoyable. Scouts pray for snow on winter campouts. But rain is never fun, especially when the temperature is around freezing. It chills one right down to the bones.

The weather was no better back at home. Mrs. Albright wished the Scouts would quit and come home early. She knew there wasn't much chance. Scouts always looked at bad weather as a challenge. In the two years the twins had been in Scouting nothing ever had been called off because of weather. Still she always could hope. She spent her time taking care of Ned, watching TV, and reading . . . but her mind always was on Ted. After she kissed Ned goodnight, she went to bed and said a little prayer for the Lord to look after the Scouts.

Meanwhile, other than the horrendous weather, the Scouts had not been doing all that bad. Supper was the big problem. It's not easy trying to start a fire with wet wood and cold fingers. Luckily, the adults had practiced the Boy Scout Motto, "BE PREPARED," and brought along a gas stove for cooking. The boys had a good hot supper and plenty of hot chocolate. The tarps had managed to keep most of the boys dry.

The leaders canceled the evening program and most of the Scouts decided to go to bed early. There's no better place to be at night on a winter campout than in a dry tent and a warm sleeping bag. Back home, Ned did not have a very good night's sleep. He kept tossing and turning. Suddenly, he looked up. In the dim light of the moon shining through the window he could see Ted sitting on the bed across the room.

"Boy, you got in late," he said, looking at his clock. "It's two-thirty in the morning. Mr. Adams call it off?"

"Be quiet," Ted responded. "You'll wake up, mom."

There was something strange about his voice.

"Ned, I've got to ask you something. Will you take care of mom? She worries a lot."

"I know. You should have seen her this weekend. But Ted, you know we'll always take care of her."

"Not we'll, Ned -- YOU! You've got to be the man of the house." "What do you mean?" Ned asked.

"Just be quiet and promise."

Ned nodded his head and promised. This was no time to be arguing anyway. They always could talk about it in the morning. "Goodnight, Ted."

"Thanks. Now go back to sleep."

The alarm went off at 7:30 in the morning. Ned looked over at Ted's bed. It was already made. This was not like Ted. Not only did he never get up this early on a Sunday morning, but he never made his bed.

'Unheard of,' thought Ned.

He got dressed and went downstairs for breakfast.

Mrs. Albright was already up. She hadn't slept too well either. On the table, there was a setting for two.

"Where's Ted?" Ned asked.

"Come on now. You know he's camping. I'm glad that rain stopped last night, but it sure was cold. I can't wait until they're home."

"But, mom, I saw . . . ."

A knock on the door interrupted Ned.

"That's probably Ted right now," Mrs. Albright replied.

She was wrong. At the door stood a Maryland State Trooper. "Mrs. Albright, I'm sorry," he said. "There's been an accident at the Scout camp. Can you come with me, please, to the County Hospital?"

She and Ned grabbed their coats and went with the trooper.

At the hospital, they met Mr. Adams, the Scoutmaster. He was in the waiting room talking to a doctor. There were tears in his eyes.

"I'm very sorry, Mrs. Albright, but there was a terrible accident at the camp last night. It was a freakish thing. The freezing rain had frozen to the trees because of the cold. Along about two o'clock in the morning, we were awakened by this crashing noise. A large tree had snapped by the shear weight of the ice and came crashing down on the campsite. It fell right on top of Ted's tent. Ted was trapped. He had caught the full force of the tree when it fell. It took several hours working with saws and axes to free him from the rubble. It was too late. He was already dead. The doctors here said he was killed instantly. There was nothing we could have done. I'm so very sorry."

The doctors took a sobbing Mrs. Albright to the side, and Mr. Adams talked to Ned.

"You're going to have to be strong now, and look after your mom," Mr. Adams said, putting his arm on Ned's shoulder.

"I know," Ned said, crying. "I already promised Ted."

THE HAND
MADE
ME DO IT

Modern medicine is wonderful. Doctors are doing things today that weren't even dreamed of when I was a boy... and doing them often. Sometimes, however, I think modern technology is moving too fast. We do too many things long before we really are ready, never realizing what the consequences of our actions might be. This is such a story.

Steve was eleven years old, but many people took him for older. He was big for his age and very athletic. He was a bundle of energy. One had to tie him down to keep him still. Steve had been a pleasure to have in the Scout troop since the day he joined. His enthusiasm and vigor was contagious and had a large impact on the other boys. I was very much saddened the day I received a phone call telling me Steve had been in a serious automobile accident. He was hurt and had been taken to the hospital.

Steve and his father were returning from a baseball game, Steve's favorite pastime, when his father lost control of the car. The car hit the curb and flipped, throwing Steve, who was not wearing his seat belt, out the door. He had escaped serious harm until the car, in one last motion, came to rest on top of his right hand. It took the rescue squad almost an hour to free Steve's hand from the wreckage. It was very badly mangled. Steve's father miraculously survived with no more than severe scrapes and bruises. They rushed Steve and his dad to the hospital.

I arrived there about an hour later. Steve's mother and father were in the waiting room. She said that the doctors were not very optimistic about Steve keeping his hand. They were in the operating room now doing their best, but most of the bones had been crushed and the muscles destroyed.

Then, the emergency room door flew open and they wheeled in another young boy. He, too, had been in an accident, however, he was in a lot worse shape than Steve. They didn't expect him to make it. Within ten minutes, he was dead. The parents of the dead boy arrived at about the same time Steve's doctors came out of the operating room. It was no use. They were going to have to remove the hand.

Quietly, the doctors moved to the other side of the room and went into a huddle. Doctors talked with doctors, and then with the parents of the dead boy. Finally, they approached us.

The doctors had an alternative to Steve losing his hand -- the transplant of another human hand. The mother of the dead boy had consented to donate her son's hand to Steve.

"Timmy never did much good in life," she said, "maybe he can do some good in death."

The operation would be risky and there would be no guarantee of success -- but there was hope. Steve's mom and dad discussed the alternatives, then gave their consent to the transplant. The operation took almost seven hours. It was very difficult, connecting the many blood vessels and muscle tissue. The operation appeared to be a success, but they wouldn't know for several months. It was going to take much exercise and rehabilitation on Steve's part.

Steve's Scout friends were a big part of his life during this period. They always were around the house -- bringing Steve his school work, helping with his exercises. Steve couldn't attend Scout meetings, so they brought Scouting to him. Steve was doing well. His determination and will power were an inspiration to everybody. He made steady progress. The doctors said that he was several months ahead of schedule on his recuperation. After eight months, Steve was allowed to return to school, and, shortly after, he was allowed to attend Scout meetings.

It was Steve's schoolwork which gave the first indication that something was wrong. Steve always was an "A" student, but suddenly his marks took a severe plunge. He barely was passing most subjects. His parents blamed the long period away from a structured school environment. Steve blamed his hand.

He said that the hand was putting the wrong answers down on the tests and not him. He was very insistent. Every time his parents would bring up the subject of grades, he would yell, "It's the hand! It's the hand!"

Finally, they took Steve to be checked by the school psychologist. It was his opinion that Steve was beginning to use his hand as a crutch -- an easy excuse for his shortcomings. He expected it would take awhile for Steve to overcome his traumatic experience and for his grades to return to normal. He cautioned the parents not to worry.

Then it happened in sports. Steve always had been one of the fastest and most accurate pitchers in the league. He was one of the best. And the rehabilitation had made him even stronger. He couldn't wait to get back to pitching. The doctors finally gave him the go-ahead. His hand was physically okay and they thought the competition would do Steve good emotionally.

Steve still was one of the fastest pitchers, but his control wasn't as good -- or was it? He'd have perfect control, and then, when the other team's best batter came up, he'd hit him with a fast ball. The opposing teams accused him of doing it on purpose. Even his coach suspected him of this and warned him about it. Steve was in tears as he swore he wasn't.

In the fifth game of the season, after two more batters were hit, Steve's coach asked him to leave the team. He was heartbroken. Again, he blamed his troubles on his hand.

"I didn't want to hit those batters. My hand made me do it!" Even at home, Steve was not acting his normal self. He always had been a very obedient, trustworthy boy. Lately, he had been sneaky and destructive. For no reason at all, he would pick up things and throw them. A neighbor accused him of painting obscenities on their fence. He denied the charges, despite two eye witnesses. His parents believed this to be a continuation of his emotional trauma and sought professional counseling again. Steve insisted that he was not doing any of these things.

"It's the hand!" he cried. "Won't anyone believe me? It's the hand!"

Thank God for Scouts. This was the last activity that Steve had that he still enjoyed . . . and then we started having our problems. First, on the campout at Elk Neck State Park, a Scout complained that someone had stolen his wallet. This is not an unusual complaint on a campout and 99 out of 100 times the wallet will turn up in the complainer's pack, neatly tucked away. Not this time.

Hank, Steve's tentmate, noticed the wallet sticking out of Steve's jacket pocket. Steve disavowed any knowledge of the wallet or how it got there.

Then, that night, we were awakened by screams coming from Steve's tent. It wasn't Steve, but Hank. He said he was awakened by this hand around his throat. Steve was strangling him. Hank had managed to knock the hand away and scream for help. Of course, Steve denied the whole thing. We moved Hank to another tent and Steve spent the night alone. Come the next morning, none of the other boys wanted to associate with Steve. He was an outcast -- a thief and a troublemaker. Steve was visibly upset.

As the Scouts were preparing breakfast, I noticed that

Steve was not around. A Scout said he had seen him a few moments ago heading for the woods with an axe. I went running in that direction.

I reached the clearing in time to see Steve place his right hand on a log and yell, "Damn you, hand. You've spoiled everything I love. I'd be better off without you!"

He raised the axe above his head to swing. I grabbed his wrist. I immediately took him home to his parents and they took him to the hospital for observation.

The hand obviously had made him go mad.

While Steve was in the hospital, I did some research. The boy, Timmy Johnson, whose hand was donated to Steve, was a classic juvenile delinquent. He was fifteen years old and had spent most of the past five years in and out of reform school. In fact, on the night he died, he had been hit by a car while running from a security guard who had seen him take some merchandise from a store. Steve's school teacher remarked that there were at least three test papers on which Steve wrote the name "Timmy" as his first name. At the time, she thought nothing of it because kids were always putting nicknames and everything else on their papers. Maybe Steve wasn't 'mad' after all. Maybe the hand was making him do things he normally would not do -- things that Timmy Johnson would! I took my findings to the doctors.

It was six months before Steve rejoined the troop. One could hardly tell the new hand was artificial -- but there was nothing artificial about the smile on Steve's face.

It was good to have the real Steve back.

JOHNNY'S BIG CATCH

This was to be a long fun-filled weekend for Troop 939. Memorial Day was here and the weather was hot. The Scouts were going to celebrate with three days and nights of camping at Chincoteague Island in Virginia. Chincoteague offers the best ocean fishing on the east coast and the boys came prepared. No sooner had the boys set up camp than they were off for the beach, fishing poles in hand. The boys hoped to get in a few hours of fishing before darkness.

For some reason the fish weren't biting today. It had been almost two hours and not a Scout had had as much as a nibble. They were just about ready to quit and go back to camp when Johnny began to scream and yell. He had a bite and it was a big one. Several other Scouts ran to his side. Sure enough, whatever was on the other end of Johnny's line was large. His pole was bent and his line was pulled taut. The Scouts took turns helping Johnny reel it in. They worked at it for almost half an hour before it finally reached shore. Suddenly their triumph turned to disappointment. There wasn't any big fish on the end of Johnny's line -- only this old sack covered with seaweed.

The Scouts dragged it up on the beach to examine it closer. This obviously was no ordinary sack. It was about five feet long and stitched closed. Evidently, somebody wanted to be sure that whatever was in the sack did not get out. Then, there was the seaweed . . . it was unlike the seaweed normally seen washed up on the beaches of Chincoteague. It contained mixtures of red and green. The boys were about to open the sack when they heard the Scoutmaster calling for them to return to camp. The Scouts dragged the sack away from the beach and hid it near the trees among the driftwood. They'd come back tomorrow and open it.

The first night at camp is always the hardest to get to sleep. The Scouts often lie in their sleeping bags and think about the things they've done or the things they're going to do. Johnny thought about his big catch. What was in the sack? He couldn't wait to open it in the morning. Johnny had a big smile on his face when he fell asleep. He didn't sleep long. He was awakened by the sound of someone, or something, walking around the campsite. He could hear the snapping of twigs and the crunching of leaves. Slowly, he stuck his head outside his tent, but he didn't see anything. Maybe it was his imagination. Since he was awake, Johnny figured he might as well go to the bathroom. His kidneys were about to burst anyway.

On his way back from the latrine, he thought he saw something move on the far side of camp. He couldn't make it out. It was in the shadows. Quietly, Johnny moved toward it. Now, it was clearer. The shadowy figure was that of a man dressed in an old-time sailor's outfit -- just like in the pirate movies he'd seen on TV. The sailor was short and had a beard. Two other things stood out. Around his neck was a gold medallion about the size of a silver dollar. In his hand was a big dagger, a knife. Johnny screamed!

The scream awoke the Scoutmaster and several other Scouts. They found Johnny alone by his tent. Johnny told everyone what he had seen and they all laughed. They had seen nothing. Johnny must have had a nightmare and walked in his sleep. The Scoutmaster helped Johnny get back into his sleeping bag and everyone else went back to their tents.

"It wasn't a nightmare," Johnny said to himself as he went back to sleep.

The next day after breakfast the Scouts went down to the beach to open the sack. What they found was not exactly what they had expected. Inside the sack were the remains of a human skeleton and the shredded rags of what probably once were clothes. The Scouts were scared -- not only of the skeleton, but also of what the Scoutmaster might do if he knew what they had found. They decided to leave the sack where it was and tell nobody. They went back to fishing, swimming, and having fun like any normal Boy Scout Troop. That night the Scouts had a big campfire. They sang songs, did skits, and, in general, enjoyed each other's company. As was customary, the Scoutmaster closed the campfire with a little story. Then, it was back to their tents and to sleep.

Johnny couldn't sleep. He kept thinking about the sailor with the dagger that he had seen the night before. He knew he hadn't been dreaming. Johnny sat in his tent and listened. He wasn't disappointed.

Along about midnight, he heard it -- the sound of someone walking through the campsite. He peeked out of his tent, and there, not ten feet away, stood the sailor. Quietly, Johnny woke up Ralph, his tentmate. This time he'd have a witness. Ralph peeked out. He, too, could see the shadowy figure of someone moving. The two boys decided to wake up the Scoutmaster whose tent was about fifty feet away. Slowly and quietly they made their way toward his tent, keeping one eye on the sailor. Suddenly, Ralph tripped. He wasn't watching where he was going. His eyes were fixed on the dagger that had just appeared in the sailor's hand. The boys froze, but the sailor didn't. He came running toward them. The moonlight reflected off the medallion -- and the dagger in the sailor's hand. Johnny and Ralph ran for the woods, screaming as loud as they could. The sailor was not far behind.

The screams awoke the Scoutmaster and the rest of the troop. Quickly, they got out of their tents and, with flashlights in hand, ran toward the noise. They found Johnny and Ralph in a small clearing not far from camp, huddled against a tree. They were almost hysterical with fright, but physically were not harmed.

After they had calmed down, they told the Scoutmaster of the sailor who had chased them into the clearing. They told of how he was ready to slit their throats with that big dagger when the noise and lights of the coming Scouts had scared him away.

The Scoutmaster and other adult leaders searched the immediate area, but saw nothing. There were no signs of the sailor. The Scoutmaster was ready to call off the search when his light caught sight of something on the ground near Johnny and Ralph. It was several large clumps of red and greenish seaweed -- still damp. This was odd. The camping area was located in the woods, well away from the beach. Also, he'd never seen this type of seaweed. The Scouts had, of course. It was the same seaweed that they had found on the sack. Guess it was time to tell the Scoutmaster about the sack. So they did.

When the sun came up, they took the Scoutmaster to the beach and showed him where they had hidden the sack containing the skeleton. The Scouts were right. The sack was covered with the same type of seaweed found in the clearing. The Scoutmaster examined the sack more closely. Inside, with the bones and rags, was an old leather pouch. Somehow, the Scouts had missed it in their haste during the earlier examination. The Scoutmaster opened the pouch and took out a small book -- a diary. It must have been the diary of the man in the sack. The man was a sailor who one night in a drunken frenzy had murdered two of his shipmates. He sneaked up on them in their sleep and slit their throats with his dagger. He was caught, put on trial, and sentenced to death. According to the law, he was to be hung and his body condemned to the sea. As the Scoutmaster was returning the diary to the pouch, a gold medallion fell to the ground.

"That's it! That's it!" screamed Johnny. "That's the medallion that the sailor had on around his neck."

The Scoutmaster realized there was only one thing to do. The body of the sailor had been condemned to the sea, and that's where it belonged. He returned all the sailor's belongings to the sack and stitched it closed. He ordered the Scouts to get a boat and make it ready. They took the sack out to deep water. There, they threw it overboard.

The last night of the campout was peaceful. Johnny and the rest of the troop slept like logs. There were no visitors, no commotion. The Scoutmaster's actions had worked. The spirit of the dead sailor was again at rest beneath the sea.

Now that I've finished my story, Kenny, tell me about that big catch of yours today.

SCOUT FROM THE PAST

Over the years we've had many strangers drop by our campfires for one reason or another, but none so strange as that night in 1975.

Our group had just completed a twelve day excursion at Philmont Scout Ranch in New Mexico. Now we were on our way to visit the Grand Canyon in Arizona before returning to Maryland. The long car ride was a pleasant change from the backpacking at Philmont. The boys relaxed and watched the scenery. Being from the east coast, the rolling hills and flowing deserts were all new to them, and they didn't want to miss a thing.

Around supper time we pulled the two vehicles off the highway onto a dirt road in an attempt to find a place to camp for the night. It wasn't long before we came to a good place. It was a large clearing, sheltered by trees, and had a stream flowing nearby for water. There was plenty of room for the ten of us. The boys set up camp while Paul and I started supper. It was nothing special, but after twelve days of dehydrated food, the boys regarded it as a feast. We ate in no time at all.

After dark, Gary started a little fire and, before we knew it, there we were, all ten of us sitting around the fire telling jokes and reminiscing about our past week's experiences. We were really enjoying ourselves.

Suddenly, out of the shadows, a man appeared. He was dressed in a fringed deerskin shirt, wore chaps on his pants, and had on boots and a cowboy hat. Other than a large, bushy moustache, his face was unrecognizable in the shadow of his big hat. He was covered with dust that he shook off before sitting on a large rock near the fire.

"He looks just like one of those Black Mountain Boys from Philmont," remarked Timmy. This was a reference to a group of wranglers who had put on a western lore demonstration at Philmont a week earlier. A few of the boys laughed, but nobody took their eyes off the stranger.

In a deep voice, the man turned and asked the boys.

"What kind of uniform is that you're wearing?"

"Scouts," they replied, "We're Boy Scouts, and these two men are our leaders," Dennis added, pointing to Paul and I.

Without turning an eye, the stranger continued, "You are not the first scouts to explore this region."

'No kidding,' I thought, 'Scouts have been camping all over the United States for the past sixty-five years.' Not wanting to be rude, however, I let him continue.

"Many years ago, Jose Hernandez, Steven Mitchell, and David Blades were Scouts in the employ of General Crook. We were tasked with finding a military supply train that was a week overdue at the fort. We outfitted ourselves with enough food, ammunition and water for several days. Our spirits were high. We were very optimistic that we could find those wagons in a very short time. We rode hard and we rode fast, just the three of us -- Jose Hernandez, Steven Mitchell, and David Blades."

The three names were repeated slowly and distinctly, as if to fix them in the memory of the boys, each of whom was now intently observing the stranger on the rock.

I, myself, wondered about this old man ... wagon trains and all that . . . but he looked friendly enough -- and the boys always were game for a good story.

The man went on.

"This country was not what it is now. There were not so many ranches. No highways. The only road you took was the road you made yourself. No stores for food. You ate what you carried, or hunted game in the mountains, or near the infrequent water holes where animals roamed. And there were Indians. Now and then they tended to be a problem.

Within a week our mission had changed from one of trying to find the supply train to one of survival. Our food supplies were running low and every day we were getting deeper and deeper into Indian territory. I marked our progress, or lack of it, in my log book.

We rode by night and hid by day, to avoid both the Indians and the intolerable heat. Sometimes, after exhausting our canteens, we were days without water, before we were able to find a water hole.

Finally, one morning as we were about to hide our horses after a hard night's ride, we were set upon by a band of Apaches. They had followed our trail up a gulch not far from here. Knowing they outnumbered us ten to one, they took none of their cowardly precautions, but came at us at full gallop, firing and yelling. Fighting was out of the question. There were too many. We quickly mounted our horses and fled up the gulch, but it was no use. The horses were too tired from the long night's ride and the Indians were gaining. We dismounted, and, taking our rifles, we ran up the slope toward a cave. We ran from rock to rock, firing our rifles as we ran. We all made it -- Jose Hernandez, Steven Mitchell, and David Blades."

"Same old crowd," a boy quipped, but the stranger ignored him and went on.

"The cave actually was a cavern about the size of a room. One man with a repeating rifle could defend the entrance against a thousand Apaches -- but against hunger and thirst, there was no defense.

Never more did we see an Indian, but we knew they were there. At night we could see their fires. For three days, watching in turn, we held out. The suffering was becoming intolerable. It was the morning of the fourth day when Jose Hernandez said, 'It is time to beat the Apaches.' Without another word, he knelt to his knees, put a pistol to his head, and pulled the trigger. It was over in a second. So he left us -- Steven Mitchell and David Blades.

He was a brave man. He knew when to die and how. It is foolish to go mad from thirst and fall from Apache bullets, or be tortured. Let us join our friend, I suggested. It was agreed. Steven Mitchell was next. He said a little prayer, and joined Jose Hernandez. I laid them out, and made one final entry in the log."

"But how did you escape?" questioned one of the boys. There was no answer.

A scream broke the silence. It was Timmy. It was coming from the woods. We ran to see what was the matter.

"I had to go to the bathroom, so I left the fire," he said. "In the light of the moon I thought I saw two men standing on the trail nearby. I could see them very clearly. It was as if they were waiting for someone. I was scared, so I screamed."

I turned to ask the stranger if he knew anything of these two men, but just as mysteriously as he had appeared, he was gone.

We threw a couple more logs on the fire and joked about the stranger. He sure was an odd fellow.

"But a darn good story teller," added Dennis. A few more jokes and it was off to our tents.

The next day as we returned to the main road, we had to stop for gas. I casually mentioned our encounter with the stranger and briefly described his story to the attendant.

"You know," the attendant stated, "years ago, they found the bodies of three men at the mouth of a cave not far from here. They had been scalped and shamefully mutilated. With the bodies they found a log book belonging to one of the men. I believe his name was David Blades."

Little did we realize that the night before, we had received the real story behind that event -- from a participant.

He was right. We were not the first 'scouts' to explore these parts.

HOME
AT
LAST

"Home."

The moaning cry swept softly through the campsite. As low as it was, it was enough to wake up Johnny Moore, a Scout from Troop 748. Johnny lay in his sleeping bag and listened. Five more times he heard it.

"Home."

He kept hoping it would stop, but it didn't.

It wasn't totally unusual to hear a cry such as this on a Boy Scout campout. Now and then, a new boy would get homesick, even on a weekend campout. But it was unusual that the leaders hadn't responded yet. They normally were up at the drop of a pin.

"Home."

The cry sounded again. Johnny decided to get up and investigate.

The moon cast a bright light over the campsite. Point Lookout State Park always was one of the troop's favorite spots. Located in Maryland on a peninsula where the Potomac River meets the Chesapeake Bay, it was the ideal place for a summer camping trip. There was good fishing, swimming, and boating -- a few of the Scout's favorite activities. The campsite itself was in the woods, away from the beach and the inlet by several miles.

"Home."

The cry was coming from the other side of the camp-site. Johnny slowly made his way toward the sound, being careful not to wake anyone else. As he approached the tents on the far side of camp, he thought it funny that the beam from his flashlight had not brought a response. He stood and waited.

"Home."

Johnny heard the cry again, but it didn't come from any of the tents. It came from the woods.

'Strange,' Johnny thought, 'there aren't any campsites located in that direction.'

Johnny cautiously made his way into the woods. Two minutes later, he heard it again.

"Home. I want to go home."

This time the cry was very clear, almost as if the person was standing next to him. He shined his light around, but saw nobody. He was standing in the middle of a small clearing surrounded by some dense brush.

"Home. I want to go home."

Again, Johnny looked and saw nothing. He was beginning to feel uneasy. Finally, Johnny turned and ran back to camp.

Johnny didn't sleep well that night. He kept having this bad dream, over and over. Someone was trapped -- trapped under a pile of dirt as if buried alive -- and he was trying desperately to get out. Johnny could remember seeing the youthful face of a boy -- a face torn in anguish.

And a uniform, or, at least, something that once was a uniform since now it was tattered and worn -- and bloody. Then, there was the low moaning cry, "Home," which echoed in the background. Johnny awoke in a sweat.

Johnny related his experiences to his Scoutmaster first thing in the morning. It was truly an incredible story. The Scoutmaster was surprised that no adults had heard the cries, and wondered if maybe Johnny hadn't dreamed the whole story.

Later that day, as the Scouts were preparing for lunch, Johnny wandered into the woods to gather firewood. Suddenly, he had this strange feeling. He became dizzy and started to sweat. Johnny dropped the firewood and headed back to camp. He began to have flashbacks of his dream -- of a young boy trying to dig out of a hole -- and the word *home* kept ringing in his head. He became totally disoriented and wandered aimlessly. Finally, something compelled him to stop. As his head cleared, he realized he was standing in the small clearing where he had heard the moaning the night before. Johnny ran to go back to camp.

A few minutes later, Johnny stopped running, only to find he was back in the clearing. Repeatedly he tried to run away, but some strange force kept bringing him back. Then, from out of nowhere, the cry rang out.

"Home. Help me go home."

Johnny fell to his knees and began digging with his hands in the soft earth. He didn't know why. He just felt compelled to do it. Within minutes, Johnny came across a badly weathered leather pouch. Carefully he opened it and looked inside where he found an old book. Johnny closed the pouch and ran back to camp to show it to his Scoutmaster.

"This looks interesting," said the Scoutmaster as he examined the leather pouch and book. It obviously was very old and had been exposed to the elements for a long time. Further examination indicated that the book was a diary. An inscription inside the cover showed that it had belonged to a Confederate soldier. But what was it doing here at this state park in the middle of nowhere. Johnny and the Scoutmaster closed the book and took it to the Park Ranger.

"Yes," the Park Ranger explained, "Point Lookout had been used by the Union during the Civil War as a Confederate prisoner-of-war camp because of its ideal location, surrounded on three sides by water. At its peak, there were over twenty thousand Confederate prisoners confined here. Unfortunately, conditions at Point Lookout were appalling and over 3500 prisoners lost their lives. Let's read the diary and see what we can find out."

Carefully turning the worn pages, they were able to figure out that the diary belonged to Private Benjamin Goode, who was an infantryman under General Longstreet. Although only fourteen years old, he had lied about his age to join the fighting. But, during his first engagement at the Battle of Gettysburg, he was captured and sent to Point Lookout. Conditions at the prisoner-of-war camp were really bad and Benjamin fast became homesick for his Virginia homeland. Thus, he planned his escape. He would do it the following night. That's where the diary ended.

The Park Ranger asked Johnny to show him the exact spot where he had found the book, since the campsite was a good distance away from where the prisoners had been confined. Johnny obliged. This sure had proved to be an interesting day.

That night, Johnny again experienced the same dream. It was so clear . . . so real. He couldn't get it out of his mind. He tossed and turned all night.

The next morning, the Park Ranger returned, along with several men with shovels. They started digging around the clearing where Johnny had made his find. It took less than an hour to find the bones -- the skeletal remains of what once had been a person. There were no clothes -- but they did find four buttons with the letters "CSA" on the front.

"Uniform buttons," said the Park Ranger, "from a Confederate uniform."

This was an extraordinary find after all these years. It appeared as if Benjamin had made good on his escape attempt, but something must have gone wrong -- perhaps he was wounded. He had made his way as far from the prisoner camp as possible, and then, perhaps hiding from the guards, died of his wounds. The years had covered and protected his bones and diary.

The Park Ranger informed Johnny and his Scoutmaster of the find. He promised Johnny the body would be given a solemn burial in the Point Lookout cemetery next to the other Civil War dead. The ranger thanked Johnny personally for his efforts.

Johnny was glad it was over. Maybe now he could sleep without those bad dreams. How wrong he was.

That night, back at home in his bed, Johnny was awakened by the young soldier's cry.

"Home. Help me go home."

This was repeated every night for a week. Johnny could do nothing to keep the cry from returning. Out of desperation, Johnny called the Park Ranger.

With the help of the Park Service, Johnny attempted to track down the home of Private Benjamin Goode. This was not an easy task since many old records had been destroyed. But Johnny and the Park Service were very determined, and the more he worked at it, the less frequent were his dreams.

Finally, the break came. The Park Service came across a letter from a young soldier in the same unit that stated he had made a new friend -- "Benjamin from Culpepper." Following this lead, the Park Service found that, indeed, a young boy named Benjamin Goode had left Culpepper to join the Confederacy in 1863, and never returned. His family had lived on a farm nearby and several ancestors still lived in the area.

The ancestors were contacted and they made arrangements to transfer the body from the Point Lookout cemetery to Culpepper, Virginia. Benjamin Goode would be buried next to his mother and father, and his two brothers and a sister, in a small church graveyard.

The Park Ranger, Johnny, and his Scoutmaster were present at the interment where the local people put on a small ceremony to welcome their hero home. As they placed the casket in the ground, Johnny could feel his burden lifted . . . and as the bugler played "Taps," Johnny heard the word *thanks* whispered in his ear.

Benjamin was home at last.

NOTES

NOTES

NOTES

NOTES

NOTES

NOTES